Chasing Bears

Chasing Bears

A CANOE COUNTRY ADVENTURE

WRITTEN AND ILLUSTRATED

BY

EARL FLECK

HOLY COW! PRESS · 1999 · DULUTH, MINNESOTA

First Printing, 1999
10 9 8 7 6 5 4 3 2

Acknowledgments: In creating the chapter illustrations of black bears, the
author drew upon the remarkable work of a number of nature photographers.
For permission to use their photographic images as models for his charcoal
drawings, he gratefully acknowledges the following: Erwin and Peggy Bauer for
Chapters 1, 2, 3 and 7; Paul Ward and Suzanne Kynaston, *Wild Bears of the
World*, Cassell plc for Chapter 4; Judd Cooney and Oxford Scientific Films for
Chapter 5; Tom and Pat Leeson for Chapter 6; ©Daniel J. Cox/
naturalexposures.com for Chapters 8 and 9; and Yschi Rue/Rue Enterprises for
Chapter 10. The lyrics for the camping song *The Border Trail*, as found in
Chapters 2 and 9, are found in *Songs of the Great Outdoors*, reprinted with
permission from Mel Bay Publications, Inc. The passage from *The Cremation of
Sam McGee*, in Chapter 7, is found in *Best Tales of the Yukon* by Robert Service,
published by Running Press.

Library of Congress Cataloging-in-Publication Data

Fleck, Earl, 1950-
Chasing bears: a canoe country adventure / written & illustrated by Earl Fleck.
p.   cm.
Summary: On a canoeing and camping trip in Canada's Quetico Provincial Park,
twelve-year-old Danny finds his strength and courage tested as he pushes
himself to keep up with his father and older brother.
ISBN 0-930100-90-5 (paperback)
(1. Canoe and canoeing Fiction. 2. Camping Fiction. 3. Quetico Provincial Park
(Ont.) Fiction. 4. National parks and reserves Fiction. 5. Canada Fiction.)
I. Title.
PZ7.F59863Ch   1999
(Fic)—dc21   99-11878
CIP

Publisher's Address:
Holy Cow! Press
Post Office Box 3170
Mount Royal Station
Duluth, Minnesota 55803

This project is supported, in part, by a grant from the Arrowhead Regional Arts
Council through an appropriation from the Minnesota State Legislature, and by
generous individuals.

Holy Cow! Press books are distributed to the trade by Consortium Book Sales &
Distribution, 1045 Westgate Drive, Saint Paul, Minnesota 55114-1065.

To my father, for taking me camping.

To Armand Ball, for the gift of Camp Widjiwagan.

*To my sons, Nathan and Justin, for daring
to go canoe camping with their father.*

Contents

chapter one

PACKING OUT

Danny Forester felt a mix of excitement and worry as he watched his father begin to stuff ten days' worth of trail food into the old canvas canoeing pack. He was excited about going along for his first canoe trip into Canada, but worried about being able to keep up with his father and older brother. Last year they had camped in the Boundary Waters Canoe Area Wilderness in northern Minnesota on what his father called a "break-in trip," but this year he had heard his father call it a "push trip"—across the U.S. / Canadian border into the canoe country wilderness of the Quetico Provincial Park in southern Ontario.

"Come on, Dan-Man, help me load the food pack."

His father had carefully arranged the trail food on the kitchen table according to meals—breakfasts, trail lunches and dinners. All of the food was either dry or freeze-dried and packed in paper, plastic or foil because no cans or bottles for food or beverages were allowed in either the Boundary Waters or Quetico wilderness regions. Yet, as Danny handed the packages of food to his father, he realized that the combined weight of all this food was beginning to add up.

"How much is the food pack going to weigh?" he asked.

His father looked up with raised eyebrows. "About a hundred pounds."

Wow, Danny thought, *how am I ever going to carry this monster?* At age twelve he weighed just over a hundred pounds himself.

Just then, Mike, Danny's eighteen-year-old brother, burst in from the garage, his muscular, six-foot four-inch frame filling the doorway. "Hey, slacker, tried on that food pack yet? You better learn to walk with that pig on your back because, if I find you face down in that big pool of muskeg on Yum Yum Portage, I might think you're just a big rock to step across on."

"Shut up, Moose!" Danny had nicknamed his big brother "Moose" after first seeing him on a football field playing tight end. With his broad shoulder pads and long legs, Mike had looked to Danny like a moose crashing through the woods.

"That's enough, boys." Danny's mother, Madeline, lifted a pan of her special voyageur bars from the oven—her own recipe from a time before anyone could buy energy bars.

Mike leaned over to Danny, placing a hand on his shoulder. "I told you, spud, you should have gone to canoeing camp instead of computer camp this summer. Just because you get straight-A's in school doesn't mean you'll even pass on the trail."

"That's quite enough, Michael." This time it was Hank, his father speaking. "I'm sure Daniel and I will have a great time in the Quetico without you," he warned without looking up from the food pack set on the floor.

Danny knew that when Mike called him "spud," he meant "sofa spud" or "couch potato," referring to the shape and condition of his body as lumpy and soft like a baked potato. Next to Mike, Danny felt flabby, fat and weak. Mike had been a three-sport letter-athlete in high school, and had been away all summer fighting forest fires in Utah and California. He looked lean and tan beneath his sun-blond crewcut hair. He never let up on Danny for his brainy interests in computers and medicine, and for not going out for sports. Danny usually looked up to his big brother, but at times like this he hated Mike.

"Don't forget the cooler food." Mike reached for the refrigerator and pulled out a block of cheese, a pound of butter, two dozen eggs and a thick slab of hickory-smoked bacon. He held the package of bacon up to his nose and inhaled loudly, smiling at Danny. "Hey, little brother, when we open this up every bear within a radius of ten miles will know we're there." Then he grabbed a milk carton block of ice from the freezer and carried the armload of cooler food and ice back out into the garage.

"Don't worry about him," Hank reassured his younger son. "He'll straighten out on the trail or I'll make him swim behind the canoe all day and sleep on rocks all night."

Danny laughed weakly, but knew that Mike had hit upon his biggest fear—his terrible fear of bears. Ever since he was a little kid he'd had nightmares about bears chasing him—huge, ferocious, snarling, attacking bears. *Bearmares,* he had named those horrible dreams, though he hadn't had one for a while.

"Here're your voyageur bars, and don't forget the first aid kit," Danny's mother reminded him. His mother was a physician who taught emergency room medicine at the University of Minnesota Medical School in Minneapolis. She had designed a special first aid training course just for Danny, and together they had assembled a comprehensive first aid kit, including inflatable splints and a plastic airway for mouth-to-mouth resuscitation. They had even created a *Wilderness Medicine* web site on the Internet. Danny had enjoyed swapping information with other first aid buffs about how to handle camping emergencies. If he felt confident about anything on the trail, it was his first aid skills. He took the plastic box with a big red cross painted on it off the kitchen table and handed it to his dad.

"Thanks, doc." Hank gave Danny a wink, then he stowed the first aid kit on the very top of all the food and rolled the plastic pack liner tightly on top of it, sealing in all the contents as protection from the water. With a grunt he tightly strapped down the top flap of the food pack. "Come on, camper, give it a try." Danny turned around as his father hefted up the monster pack and helped him get his arms into the shoulder straps. "Now take it outside."

"Uff," Danny groaned, and let out a little laugh. The pack nearly crushed him to the floor, but he steadied himself, vowing to show Mike he could do it. He staggered headlong out through the screen door and into the garage.

Outside he could see that Mike had lined up all of their camping equipment next to the old red Chevy Suburban parked in the driveway. "Awesome!" Mike exclaimed, pumping his fist up and down, then grabbing the pack off of Danny's shoulders. "I dub thee pack—The Crusher!" He set the monster down next to a much lighter personal pack containing sleeping bags, clothing and rainwear, and an equipment pack. Three paddles, each a different length, and each with a different Native American pictograph of an animal painted on the blade, were leaning against the Suburban along with three red life jackets.

Danny's father came outside with a small rucksack of his own. He held an equipment checklist in his hand and surveyed the pile of gear next to the truck. Danny could sense the intensity of his father's excitement about the trip. At no other time did his father seem quite as alive, quite as enthused about life as when he was packing out for a canoe trip.

"What about the cook kit?" He looked at Danny.

"Oh, yeah, I forgot." Danny scooted back into the house. On the floor of the kitchen near the back door he found the old heavy aluminum cook kit—three open pots with lids nested together, a coffee pot, two fry pans with handles and six flat plates. Inside the coffee pot three old green plastic cups were stacked together with three stainless steel sierra cups. All except the sierra cups were the original pieces of the cook kit. And the cook kit, Danny knew, was among the most cherished of his father's belongings, for his father had told him the story of how he had come into possession of this family treasure.

Hank Forester had grown up as the adopted and only child of a log cabin carpenter and a rural school teacher in the lake region of southern Ontario, near White Otter Lake. His father, Danny's grandfather, had also been a builder of wooden canoes, among the finest ever made, white cedar ribs and planking, eighteen-footers with four extra inches of freeboard—called simply White Otter canoes. Each could easily handle six hundred pounds of gear and provisions for two paddlers, and hold steady in rough waves or heavy rapids.

Hank's father had taken him canoe camping all throughout the region. And once, when Hank was eighteen, they had even canoed three hundred and fifty miles down the Seal River to Hudson Bay. But the day after returning from

Hudson Bay, on a Sunday morning in late summer, Hank and his parents came home from church to find their log home engulfed in flames, including his father's canoe building workshop. All of their canoeing and camping equipment was destroyed in the fire, except for the one White Otter canoe they had paddled to Hudson Bay. They had set it out in the sun to dry the water-soaked canvas skin. And, next to the canoe sat the old aluminum cook kit Hank had scrubbed clean and set out to dry as well.

After the fire had been extinguished, Hank's father stood with him beside the charred remains of their home. He pointed to the canoe and the cook kit and said to Hank, "These are yours now, son. I have nothing else to pass on to you." He never built another canoe. That fall Hank went off to college to study history and painting. His parents moved to Toronto. Both of them had died before Danny ever knew them.

But the cook kit lived on, and Danny had been entrusted with its care. His father had told him, "I want you to be in charge of the cook kit on this trip. I know you can handle the responsibility. No dents in the bottom from banging it on rocks. No pots sinking to the bottom of the lake. Understand?" Danny had nodded his head in agreement. Inside the kitchen he grabbed the rope tie for the canvas bag that contained the old cook kit, lifted it up and ran back outside.

"Okay, let's load up the canoe." Hank directed Mike. It was well after dark. Hank and Mike had already stowed the packs, cooler, paddles and life jackets in the back of the Suburban. They were inside the lighted second garage with Danny's mother, and Rachel, Danny's eight-year-old little sister. On a canoe rack built against the inside wall sat the last of the White Otter canoes, the one Hank and his father had paddled to Hudson Bay, the deep eighteen-footer painted navy blue with a moose pictograph painted in white on the bow.

"Easy now, no scratches." Hank with the stern and Mike with the bow eased the big blue canoe down off the rack, carried it outside and centered it on top of the Suburban where they strapped it down tightly across its belly and secured the bow and stern with nylon ropes tied to the front and rear bumpers.

Danny set the cook kit inside the truck, then he double-checked his pockets—Swiss army knife and plastic whistle on the end of a lanyard in his right pants pocket, waxed matches and a flint and steel fire starter in his left pants pocket along with a mini-first aid kit. In his right shirt pocket he had crammed a compact foil blanket for an emergency shelter, and in his left shirt pocket three Snickers bars fit snugly side by side. On another lanyard around his neck hung his red ten-in-one compass device next to a miniature flashlight; and inside the band of his hat he had hidden a coil of fishing line with three hooked plastic leeches. Food, fire, first aid, shelter—all stuffed in his pockets in case of an emergency. He was ready for anything.

"I'm envious of you guys. I wish I was going along." Danny knew his mother was sincere. She and his father had met at a youth camp in northern Minnesota. She had been the camp physician and he had been the summer trail director, after a number of summers working as a trail guide. They both loved the northwoods, and they had married at the camp in September at the end of their second summer together. For their honeymoon, they had paddled and portaged the length of the Quetico from Cache Bay on Lake Saganaga in the east to Beaverhouse Lake in the west.

"I want to go too," Rachel begged.

"I wish you could come along." Hank gave Madeline a kiss, then lifted Rachel up for a big hug. "Maybe next year to the Boundary Waters with you," and he set her down.

Danny felt a bit awkward. Standing between his father and his brother and his mother and his sister, he didn't quite know what to do or how to feel. Again he felt caught between excitement and fear, adventure and danger, warm security and cold risk. Then both his mother and Rachel grabbed him for a hug and a kiss on each cheek.

"You be careful," his mother whispered. "Stick with your father and your big brother, stay together on the portages, wear your life jacket and remember all that I've taught you. Remember S.T.O.P. if there's trouble—Stay-Think-Organize-Plan." Danny nodded his head. "Now, come on. I want a picture of the three of you," she said more loudly.

Danny, Mike and Hank lined up beside the Suburban with the canoe on top, Danny in the middle, his pockets bulging. They were already dressed in their trail clothes—oiled boots, patched jeans, old flannel shirts and each wearing a different hat. Hank, at six-feet six-inches and two hundred and forty pounds, stood taller and heavier than Mike. This somehow pleased Danny, and gave him some feeling of security—to know that there was still someone to keep Mike in check in his worst moments of teasing. Still, standing there pressed between the two of them, Danny felt like a loaf of white bread squashed between two towering timbers. *How will I ever keep up with these guys?* he asked himself.

"Smile," his mother called out as the camera flashed. Then Mike climbed into the front passenger seat while Danny positioned himself in the middle of the second seat. Out the open windows of the Suburban they watched as their parents exchanged a few private words. Danny was always struck by the lightness of his mother, with her nearly white-blond hair and fair, youthful-looking skin, up against the darkness of his father with his coal black hair and dark, weathered features. Madeline held a cellular phone in her right hand, gesturing with it as she talked to Hank.

"Watch," Mike whispered to Danny, "she wants him to take the cell phone in case there's trouble, but I betcha' he won't take it." They tried not to stare as their father shook his head, leaned over and gave their mother a quick peck on the cheek, then turned toward the truck. "See, I told you. Dad's what you call a purist."

To Danny, Mike seemed rather proud of this assessment of their father. He didn't tell Mike that he thought a cellular phone might not be such a bad idea. *What if a bear steals our food pack? Or what if I get appendicitis? Or what if I chop the ax into my foot?* His thoughts raced ahead, but he knew he couldn't ask his father all these questions again for fear of hearing, "I'm not going to play *what if* with you tonight, Danny. It's time to *just do it.*" Sometimes his father lost patience with him, with all of his fears, and he forced him to try something new, even if he was afraid.

"Come on, Rachel, let's say good-bye to the boys." Danny heard his mother call out.

"You mean good-bye to—the men!" Mike smiled and slapped his hand against the truck door.

"Yeah—the men!" Danny chimed in less convincingly, in a boy's voice that had not yet deepened.

Hank slid into the driver's seat, started the engine and backed out of the driveway as everyone continued to wave and shout their good-byes. They would drive up north in the night and arrive at the departure point for their canoe trip in the morning.

chapter two

UP NORTH

S oon they were heading north, the lights of the city
fading into the darkness behind them, the stars shining
brighter and brighter against the black night sky ahead of
them. Danny sat in the middle of the second seat of the
roomy Suburban, leaning forward with his forearms resting
on the back of the front seat. As he drove, his father drank
hot, strong-smelling coffee from an old plastic thermos, while
Danny and Mike drank thick, sweet hot chocolate from their
own stainless steel thermos bottles. They knew it was useless
to argue with their father about which radio station to listen
to as he tuned into public radio news. It was the second week
in September. Mike would begin his first year of college after
their return, but Danny's junior high school had already
started. His parents had made special arrangements for him
to miss a week of school.

"All right, tell me, Danny, what do you have to do for each of your classes?" His father wanted to know.

"All I have to do for English is keep a journal. My math teacher wants me to keep track of the distances we cover in different units of measurement, and maybe some map and compass readings for extra credit. For history I have to write a report about either the first peoples or the voyageurs who lived or traveled along the border lakes. Science can be almost anything, so I thought I'd keep track of all our wildlife sightings, and maybe a list of different trees. For art we're doing a photography unit, so I'll try some nature shots, or maybe we can find some pictographs. I can make up anything else I miss when I get back."

"What about Phy. Ed.?" It was Mike asking.

He would have to ask, Danny thought to himself, resentfully. He hated Phy. Ed. more than anything. *Pull-ups, ugh.* He couldn't even do one pull-up. "Mr. Jones said that canoeing in the Quetico would be like an all-day workout every day I'm on the trail, and he'd give me an A if I just made it back alive." The first part was true, but Danny lied a little about the "A" part.

"If you make it through this trip and carry even just the personal pack across every portage, I'll vouch for you with Coach Jones." Mr. Jones had been Mike's football coach. "Anything less gets you an F." Mike laid down his challenge. Danny wasn't sure whether or not he was kidding.

"Okay, pop quiz." Mike fired the questions back to his little brother. "The only three things allowed to touch the bottom of the canoe?"

"Water, air and bread dough." Danny knew all the answers, but played along.

"Sharp rocks just below the surface of the water?"

"Lake sharks."

"Submerged logs just below the surface of the water?"

"Dead heads."

"Lumies?"

"Aluminum canoes."

"TL?"

"Trail lunch."

"TP?"

"Toilet paper."

"Lumberjack TP?"

"Large-leafed aster."

"PB?"

"Peanut butter."

"BJ?"

"Bug juice."

"What do we do if we swamp?"

"Stay with the canoe."

"And why do we go camping in September?"

"No bugs! No people! Great fishing! Yes!" Pumping his right fist in the air with his sons, Hank enthusiastically joined in on the game, then burst forth with one of his favorite camp songs:

> *"It's the far northland that's a calling me away,*
> *as take I with my packsack to the road.*
> *It's the call on me of the forest in the north,*
> *as step I with the sunlight for my load."*

Sitting there, between yet behind his father and brother, Danny felt a part of something very special, but he wasn't sure yet if it was as important to him as it was to them. He sat back in his seat. It was late, near midnight, and he had been up early that day. Soon, with the hot chocolate in his stomach and the drone of the tires on the pavement, he laid his head down on the cook kit next to him and fell into a deep, but uneasy sleep.

Struggling mightily along the muddy, rain-slicked portage trail, he had lost sight of Mike and his father. The straps of the crusher food pack cut so deeply into his shoulders that his hands and arms had gone completely numb. Sharp rocks and gnarled tree roots battered his already bruised and blistered feet, even though he wore his trail boots. His rain jacket felt like a portable sauna as sweat poured off his face.

In the middle of a stand of young birch trees, the trail leveled off and widened into a smelly and ominous-looking pool of muskeg. Someone had constructed a bridge-like path using thin white birch logs laid down corduroy fashion along one side of the muskeg hole, but the footing was unsteady at best. The smooth thin logs rolled and shifted unpredictably as he inched his way along the path. He tried to grab ahold of the standing trees to keep his balance, but his hands were too numb.

Head bent down, straining, he kept his eyes focused on every step in front of him—so he didn't see the huge black bear rearing up on her hind legs in front of him, or hear her two cubs squealing for their mother behind him—until it was too late! He had come between a mama bear and her cubs! At first he just froze, then her ferocious growl knocked him off his feet and he fell backwards, pack first, into the muskeg. He remained stuck, pinned down by the weight of the food pack, flailing his arms and legs in the air and screaming like a trapped animal. The enraged bear growled at him ever more angrily, swiping the air with her huge clawed paws.

"Help!" Danny cried out in his sleep. "Help! Help! Help!"

"Easy, little buddy, take it easy." Hank gently shook Danny awake. "It's just one of your bearmares. You'll be okay." Mike was driving.

Just one of my bearmares, Danny thought to himself. *Where were you guys on the portage?* He felt embarrassed despite his father's reassurance.

"Pull in down here." Hank directed Mike with a gesture. Mike slowed the truck, turned down into a wayside rest area along the lake shore highway and shut off the engine. "Let's check it out."

The three voyageurs stepped out onto the smooth pebble beach along the south shore of a bay. In the darkness Danny could hear the gently lapping waves against the rocks, feel the cool, almost chilly breeze against his face, and smell the distinctive scents of the great lake.

"Look there." Hank pointed to the northern sky. Streaks of light, red, yellow, green, shot up from the dark horizon and danced together and apart. The northern lights shone brilliantly, clearer than Danny had ever seen them from the cities. He stood motionless, hands in his pockets, looking up in awe without speaking.

Mike, searching with a small flashlight, had found a huge driftwood log and sat on it holding open two paper bags. While Danny had been sleeping in the back seat of the truck, his father and brother had stopped at the Beaver Lodge Bait Shop along the north shore of the great lake, where right beside the leeches and nightcrawlers they also sold cheddar cheese curds and smoked fish. Danny and his father joined Mike on the log.

"What could be finer?" Mike mused as he held out the open bags for his father and brother, "Lake Superior at my feet, Aurora Borealis overhead, the taste of cheddar cheese and smoked lake trout in my mouth and the world's best canoeing buddies at my side." He gave Danny a friendly nudge with his elbow.

Danny thought there might be hope for Mike after all. He popped a cheese curd into his mouth and broke off a piece of smoked fish.

"Watch out for fish bones," Hank cautioned. But that was

all he had to say as the three of them sat there for a long while in silence—watching the northern lights until they nearly faded, inhaling the smells of what to them was the greatest of lakes, listening to the waves upon the shore and the wind in the trees. Danny suspected it was the wind in the trees that got his father moving.

"Time to go." Hank stood up. "Rosco said he'd have a lumberjack breakfast ready for us at six, and we want to get across Sag before the wind comes up." Danny understood that "Sag" was short for Lake Saganaga, a spectacular lake, legendary for its record-sized walleyes. Sag was the big water, the dangerous water they would have to cross to enter into Canada and the Quetico Provincial Park.

Inside the Suburban, Mike held up three cartons of nightcrawlers for Danny to see. "One dozen for each of us," he smiled. "The smallies will be jumping into the canoe." Then he held up a clear plastic oxygen pack containing three dozen huge black leeches. "But these," he grinned, opening his eyes even wider, "are for the walleyes."

"Wow!" Danny burped up some smoked fish in his excitement. "When can we go fishing?"

"I've got a spot in mind for tonight." Hank pulled the truck back out onto the highway, turned the heater on low to take the chill off and, with his sons, headed further north along Highway 61.

Danny fired fishing questions at Mike until his big brother tired of answering and fell asleep with his head against the door. Then no one talked for a long time, but Danny couldn't fall asleep again. He wondered how his father could stay awake all night as they passed through mile after mile of forest. But he knew his father had often stayed awake all night, sometimes for days on end, feverishly painting in his studio. His father was a painter and a teacher of painting, but for the past year he had been home on some kind of a leave from work—a "sabbatical" his father called it, a time to work on his own art.

But Danny hadn't seen a finished painting in over two years; and it seemed to him like his father spent too much time sleeping and watching television. Once he had over-heard his parents arguing in their bedroom—something about a medication his father didn't want to take, complaining that it killed his creativity. His mother insisted that he take the medication—for his "mood swings" she called it.

When Danny asked his mother why his father wasn't working, she reminded him that his father was an artist and that sometimes artists go into a kind of hibernation. He would come out of it, like a bear awakening in the spring, she reassured Danny. But secretly, he worried about his father. He was happy to see him so excited about their camping trip.

An hour or so later Hank pulled over again, this time at a high scenic cliff-side rest stop overlooking Lake Superior. "Look there," he said quietly to Danny, pointing to the northeast.

Ahead of him, through the windshield of the Suburban, Danny could see the lights of a small lake shore village. A full yellow moon rested just above the town as if to welcome them.

"That's Grand Marais. From there we head uphill away from the lake, up the Gunflint Trail Highway another sixty miles to Rosco's place."

"What's a lumberjack breakfast?" Danny asked.

"You'll see." Hank poured himself another cup of black coffee. "Now why don't you try to get a little more sleep. We've got a big day ahead of us."

Danny laid his head back down on the cook kit and closed his eyes. The old canvas bag smelled like wood smoke. As he drifted off, he imagined the campfires he would build on this trip with his father and his brother—fires to warm them and cook their food, fires to tell stories around and watch burn for their multicolored beauty, and fires to keep the bears away.

Though it felt like he had been asleep for only a few minutes, it must have been an hour or more when he heard the beep of the horn and his father call out, "Rosco!"

Danny opened his eyes to see his father step out of the truck and into the laughing bear hug of a massive, bearded, wild-looking man wearing tattered bib overalls, a red flannel shirt and a greasy baseball cap that read: ROSCO'S CANOE COUNTRY OUTFITTERS. Both men patted each other on their backs.

"Hank Forester, good to see you, my man." Hank and Rosco Knute had both guided canoe trips out of the youth camp twenty years earlier, and Rosco had been the best man at Hank and Madeline's wedding on chapel point at the camp. "And I see you brought a couple of lily-dippers along with you this year."

Danny and Mike stumbled from the truck, both shivering in the pre-dawn chill of the northern pine forest—trees all around. Danny could still taste the cheese curds and smoked fish in his mouth.

"Hey, guys." Rosco gave off an odor of fish guts and wood smoke as he shook each of their hands. "I hope you gunwale-bangers are hungry, because I cooked up a whole lotta' food."

Danny felt even punier standing next to this bear of a man—nearly as tall but twice as wide as his father. *What an animal,* he thought. *He must weigh four hundred pounds.* And he felt a bit apprehensive, like being led to the castle by the giant, as he followed the men toward Rosco's lodge. *Lily-dippers? Gunwale-bangers? What's with the name calling?*

But the warmth and smells of Rosco's canoe country kitchen felt good as they sat down around a huge hewn log table to a breakfast feast the likes of which Danny had never seen before—a platter heaped with plate-sized sourdough pancakes slathered with whipped butter, pitchers of real maple and homemade blueberry syrup, more platters piled high with Canadian bacon, fried eggs and hash browns, plus a pan of hot cinnamon rolls, freshly frosted. Danny wondered what his mother, the cholesterol-counting physician, would have to say about Rosco's breakfast spread; but he loved this kind of food, and so when Hank gave the nod, the grub began to fly off the platters and into their mouths having barely landed on their plates.

Rosco moved back and forth between his massive black stove and the log table, a pot of hot coffee in one hand and a pitcher of hot cocoa in the other.

"Did your dad tell you why this is called a lumberjack breakfast?" Both Danny and Mike shook their heads, their mouths too full to answer. Rosco laughed. "Exactly. Back in the old days the lumberjacks had to eat as much as they could in as short a time as possible so they could get out to work—so, they never bothered to talk at breakfast." He laughed again.

"So, how was your summer, Rosco?" Hank asked as he cut through another stack of cakes.

"Aw, terrible, just terrible." Rosco shook his head. "Plenty of business, but all the wrong types. Not like the old days. Bunch of gearheads these days. High tech. You should see the goofy equipment some of these people pack in—little espresso makers, laptop computers, fish finders. On a canoe trip! Can you believe it? And the latest thing, these GPS devices—Global Positioning Systems—and cell phones. Might as well not leave the office." Danny looked at Mike, who was smiling, his cheeks stuffed with bacon. *GPS*, Danny remembered, *why didn't I think of that? We could pinpoint our longitude and latitude within a hundred feet and call it in on the cell phone.* Was he the only one in Rosco's kitchen who could see the wisdom in this?

The giant ranted on. "Everyone's afraid to get their feet wet. Everyone wants lightweight this and lightweight that. Trail cooking means boiled water poured into a bag of freeze-dried gourmet food. Most of 'em never heard of a reflector oven, or a wood-canvas canoe like that treasure there on top of your truck. Bunch of lily-dipping, gunwale-banging gearheads!" Rosco slammed down the coffee pot. "Who wants more cakes?" He held up the platter.

All three of his guests pushed their palms away, pleading for mercy beneath Rosco's avalanche of food; but his avalanche of words continued.

"Why, I went out to check on one group camped on Red Rock Bay. Found them easy enough, just followed the soap suds across the lake. Caught 'em all shampooing their hair in the rapids; and after I had emphasized to them not to let one drop of soap touch the lake. Well, they got their flaps jacked plenty hot that day. If they can't abide by a few simple rules, common courtesy, and keep these waters clean, then I don't want their business. Bunch of knuckle-headed gunwale-bangers, all of 'em. You can hear 'em two lakes away, banging the shafts of their paddles against the gunwales with every stroke. Drives me nuts. I'm glad to have 'em all outta' here and have the silence of September back."

"Amen!" Hank jumped in.

The growling, red-faced bear-man grabbed the pot of coffee in one hand and the pitcher of cocoa in the other. But Hank set his cup upside down on the table, stood up and put his arm around Rosco's shoulder. "We are thankful for the great hospitality of our old friend Rosco Knute, but we gotta' get going before the wind kicks up on Sag."

Danny felt so stuffed he couldn't imagine how he would be able to paddle. "Yeah, thanks," he said, standing up.

"Me, too," said Mike, grabbing a last piece of bacon.

"You'll thank me later for the carbo-load, fuel for the journey." Rosco smiled. "And especially if you want to grow up to be a big guy like your dad, you gotta' eat big."

"Ah, yeah." Danny looked to his dad, but Rosco put his arm around his shoulder as they walked out the door.

"Lemme' tell you about the time your father and I took Poohbah from the south in May."

"Another time, Rosco," Hank interrupted. "I'm serious, we gotta' get across Saganaga before the wind hits. I didn't like what I heard last night coming out of the northwest."

"Ya, I suppose you're right." Rosco finally gave in. "Come on, I'll drive you to the boat landing."

Outside, the rising sun had just peeked above the jagged tree line to the east and begun to burn the mist off the lake. Danny found a path down to Rosco's dock. Not twenty yards out on the lake he spotted a pair of loons swimming, their shiny black heads just out of the water. He watched quietly, and in a moment one of the loons opened its mouth and let out a soft low tremolo call as if to welcome Danny to the northwoods; and Danny understood in that moment, that they had driven through the night, as if in a dream, and come to arrive at that place they all called, "Up North."

chapter three

CROSSING SAGANAGA

D anny felt a surge of excitement as he ran up from the dock and climbed back into the Suburban. Mike pushed in beside him. Rosco chuckled as he pulled his massive weight into the front passenger seat, causing the whole truck to lean to one side. Hank drove. A mile or so up the road, the Gunflint Trail Highway ended at a U.S. Forest Service campground. A sandy boat landing on tiny Gull Lake would serve as the departure point for their water route.

To Danny, everyone except him seemed to know what to do without being told. His father jumped out of the truck and headed over to a Forest Service permit station. They wouldn't be camping overnight in the U.S. Boundary Waters, so a self-issued day permit would suffice for passing through the Boundary Waters Canoe Area Wilderness, called the BWCAW, on their way to and return from the Canadian waters. No other campers were around.

Mike and Rosco hurriedly untied the canoe and lifted it off the truck. Then they walked it into the water and set it belly down. This was the method with a wood and canvas canoe—only water, air and bread dough touched the canvas skin—no running it up on the rocks. Danny's father called it "wet-boot camping."

"Come on! Come on!" Mike gestured impatiently to Danny. Quickly, he grabbed the cook kit and walked into the water up to his knees. The water was colder than he had expected as his socks and lower pants legs soaked up the lake. Mike stowed the cook kit under the stern seat. "It always goes here," he looked at Danny. "That way if we swamp it won't fall out, and the sternsman can always check it paddling away from the portage to make sure we haven't forgotten it." Danny was reminded of the importance of his cook kit assignment.

"Here, put these on." Hank handed a life jacket to each of his sons. "Please your mother." Mike frowned and pulled his on without latching it. Danny double-checked his bulging shirt pockets, then he tightly buckled the front straps of his personal floatation device, or his PFD as he liked to call it. Hank set his rucksack behind the stern seat on top of the cook kit.

Rosco joined the wet-boot campers in the water, personal pack in one hand, equipment pack in the other. "I got your bait snug on top the equipment pack." Mike grabbed the personal pack and Hank grabbed the equipment pack, stowing them in the stern compartment of the eighteen-footer.

"Come on, Dan-Man, grab the paddles." Danny and his father hustled back to the truck. From the back of the Suburban, Hank dumped out the cooler water and ice, then found room in the food pack for the cheese, eggs, bacon and butter.

Danny understood that the food would keep well enough in the cool autumn weather, but more importantly—coolers were not a part of any canoe trip his father would ever lead.

He grasped the three paddles with both hands as his father groaned with the weight of the food pack, and the two of them walked back into the water. Mike lifted the monster pack off his father's back and set it in the most forward part of the stern compartment, just behind the yoke.

Rosco produced a bag of his fresh-baked cinnamon rolls. He handed them to Mike. "Okay, campers, save some fish for me." He shook hands with Danny and Mike, then wrapped another bear hug around Hank, the men patting each other on their backs.

"Ten days, right back here, about noon." Rosco nodded that he understood Hank's instructions. Then Hank turned to his sons. "Mike, you duff. Danny, take the bow."

Danny was surprised that his father had chosen him first to paddle bow. He could feel his excitement rising even higher. He and his father held the canoe steady as Mike climbed in the middle bow compartment, centering himself low in the duffer's position and stowing his paddle beside him.

"You next," his father nodded. Danny laid his paddle across the bow, gripped opposite gunwales with both hands and concentrated on stepping in the very center of the canoe, along the keel screws, as he eased himself into the bow seat. Then Hank straddled the stern seat, draining the water off his boots before tucking his feet beneath him. And just like that, quietly in the light of an early September morn, with a nod and a wave from Rosco the bear-man, they were off—floating, paddling, gliding toward the Seagull River and Lake Saganaga.

Paddling bow first in the big blue canoe felt like a special privilege to Danny. He had learned to appreciate the beauty of his grandfather's craftsmanship, for he had often heard his father talk about how a kind of golden light seemed to glow from within the wood itself—wide planking just an eighth of an inch thick, and ribs just a quarter of an inch thick. He, too, could see this light in the wood. And he had heard his father talk about how the golden-colored wood held the heat of its days standing tall in the sun, and thus it gave off a kind of warmth to the paddler. This, too, felt true for Danny as he sat comfortably in the bow seat surrounded by the light and warmth of the varnished cedar, dipping his paddle into the cold water.

"Don't forget to feather your paddle," Mike barked from behind him, reminding Danny to always bring his paddle forward flat against the water. "And remember, the bowman provides sixty-five percent of the power. I wanna' see some major whirlpools coming off the ends of your strokes. No lily-dipping."

Shut up, Moose, Danny thought to himself, but tried to paddle harder and faster as the canoe's keel caught the current of the Seagull River flowing out of Gull Lake through a rocky narrows toward Saganaga. The Seagull River was little more than a channel a couple of miles long between the two lakes. Yet it had enough of a current, and Danny had learned that canoeists had to keep up with the speed of the current to maintain control of their vessel.

After a few minutes Hank spoke up. "Danny, relax. You're paddling way too fast for me. I can't keep up with you. Remember, I take long strokes myself, so it's better if you take longer, slower bow strokes. We gotta' find our rhythm, and we gotta' pace ourselves. It's going to be a long day."

Danny slowed down and tried to pull his paddle longer, farther back in the water. Then, up ahead he spotted a few riffles in the water indicating rocks. He immediately dropped down onto his knees in the "shotgun" position, the blade of his paddle tucked under his armpit with the shaft pointed forward and the grip just beneath the water off the bow of the canoe—ready to ward off any rocks. It was the bowman's job to avoid any lake sharks or dead heads. But the channel was wide enough and clear of boulders as they scooted through the riffles.

"Good job," Hank called out.

Danny sat back in the bow seat, and rather more quickly than he had imagined, the short stretch of river widened and widened. The rocky, tree-lined river bank turned into the rocky, tree-lined shore and the tree-covered islands of Lake Saganaga. They were headed due north, and as the sun burned off the morning mist Danny marveled at the intensity of the blue sky above them—a more intense blue color than he had ever seen in the cities. He also noticed the wind.

"Switch!" His father called out, and on the count of three they switched sides, always paddling on opposite sides, stroke for stroke, their paddles entering and leaving the water at precisely the same instant as the long keel sliced through wave after wave, never breaking their momentum. All the while, Hank hummed some old voyageur tune.

Even with his wet feet, Danny felt hot beneath his life jacket. He pulled off his trail hat. He realized that this truly was going to be an all day workout. Before long, though, he caught sight of the red maple leaf on the white background of the Canadian flag. Their first stop, the Canadian Customs Station, sat on Red Pine Island perhaps a quarter of a mile ahead—and it was only nine o'clock in the morning. Except for the distant drone of a motor, they seemed to be the only boat on the lake.

"Watch for the chain, now, Danny." Mike spoke with a distinct sense of urgency. "This is your first crossing over the border."

For years, Danny had heard his father and brother talk about the long red and white chain that was stretched underwater across the lakes along the border between the United States and Canada, and how special it was to catch a glimpse of this chain when you crossed over into Canada. He knew it was a lie, a tall tale, but he could never get them to admit it. So as Lake Saganaga opened up to his right and to his left, and as they crossed into Canadian waters, he kept his eyes on the deep, sky-blue waters ahead of him.

"Hey, is that a bald eagle sitting on top of that tallest white pine over there?" Mike sounded even more excited.

"Where?" Danny looked up, toward the tree line.

"Guess not." Mike now sounded disappointed.

"Wow, there it is!" Now it was Hank, sounding excited from the stern. "The chain!"

Danny turned around. His father pointed with the blade of his paddle to the wake behind the canoe. "Guess you missed it. It's back there, and it looks like they gave it a fresh coat of paint, too."

"Let's turn back," Danny pleaded.

"Nope. Too late. No turning back." Hank shook his head. "You shoulda' been paying attention rather than looking for eagles. Now paddle."

Mike shrugged his shoulders and shook his head too. "Guess you missed it, kid."

"You guys are lame, totally lame." Danny stabbed his paddle into the water and pulled back as hard as he could. The Canadian Customs flag flapped in the wind just a couple of hundred yards ahead of them.

The customs agent, a woman in a white uniform shirt and black slacks, met the travelers at the dock. Danny and his father followed her into the customs station house while

Mike stayed with the canoe. The big red-on-white maple leaf flag flapped loudly overhead, predicting a windy crossing.

Inside the white wood-frame building Hank Forester answered a few questions. No firearms. No felony convictions. Their planned length of stay in Canada would be nine nights and ten days, all in the Quetico Provincial Park—for two American citizens and himself, "still a son of Canada," he announced. The customs agent seemed pleased to learn that Danny's father had retained his Canadian citizenship. She stamped their entry permit and escorted them back out to the dock.

"Nor'wester headed in." She nodded in the direction of the park. "Better get across Sag as quick as you can."

"Don't we know it." Hank too looked in the direction of the park where an occasional whitecap could be spotted out on the big lake.

Mike was sitting on the edge of the dock holding the canoe steady with his legs as it bobbed up and down with the waves. He had pulled out their rain jackets and rain pants from the top of the personal pack, which Danny couldn't understand because the sky was clear. "Better put these on, little brother, they'll keep you warm. It's your turn to duff."

Hank pulled a big sponge tied to a cord out of the front pouch of the equipment pack, then he leaned over and tied one end of the cord to the bow thwart just behind the bow seat, dropping the sponge into the bottom of the canoe where the duffer sat. "Get in," he said to Danny. "We'll hide behind islands as long as we can, but eventually we'll have to turn into the wind and cross this big open stretch." He showed Danny the map of Lake Saganaga. "If we take on water, you're in charge of bailing. Use this sponge."

Danny's father had a way of looking directly into his eyes when he was most serious. Danny pulled on his rain jacket and rain pants and stepped down into the canoe, settling into the duffer's position. He was secretly relieved to get a break from paddling, but he felt a bit apprehensive about what exactly his father meant by the words, "take on water."

Mike climbed into the bow and Hank took the stern. They moved confidently away from the dock, each with a nod to the customs agent. They were still relatively sheltered from the wind as they swung back in a southwesterly direction. At first this seemed like backtracking to Danny, but it made sense after his father explained how they would hide in the lee sides of a string of islands until they absolutely had to turn into the northwest wind and cross the open water. For canoeists, it was better either to hide from the wind or paddle directly into the wind. Canoes were not designed for taking on wind and waves at an angle.

An hour later they had run out of islands and, without so much as a pause, Hank and Mike maneuvered the heavily-loaded canoe out into the big waves. Danny sat eye-level with the whitecaps, feeling like he was more in the water than on top of the water. And as the bow turned directly into the northwest wind, Mike shouted over his shoulder, "Remember to hang onto the canoe if we swamp!"

Danny just tried to stay centered as the first big wave hit. He could actually feel it roll beneath the canoe, raising the bow into the air before it crashed back down onto the next crest of a wave. His heart jumped a bit and he let out a nervous laugh, hoping no one heard. But by then the wind and the sound of the bow hitting wave after wave had drowned out all talk.

Two miles of open water lay before them. Their goal was to reach the shelter of the northern shoreline, a dark tree line off in the distance. Mike and his father had worked out a signal, and switched sides after every ten strokes. And though at first it seemed as if the waves might just push them backwards across the lake, smashing them into the rocks along the south shore, slowly, ever so slowly, they gained on the lake—Saganaga—a true northwoods lake— dark, deep, and dangerous.

SPLASH! SPLASH! SPLASH! The biggest waves advanced in sets of three, like combination punches, some throwing the bow so high up in the air that Mike's next stroke would touch only sky. And at times, Danny feared the canoe itself might break apart. How could any vessel so fragile against the rocks be so strong against the waves?

SPLASH! SPLASH! SPLASH! Up and down, the waves grew bigger and bigger with a wind that had now come up full force as they paddled harder and harder across the lake. Now, instead of slicing through the waves, they were paddling up one side and down the other side of each consecutive wave— a bad sign. Then Danny heard Mike yell out, "Hang on!" And with a whoosh, the next giant wave washed completely over the bow, drenching Mike from the waist down and dumping part of the lake into the bottom of the canoe.

Still, Hank held steady in the stern, yelling to Danny, "Bail! Grab the sponge! Squeeze it out over the side!"

Danny quickly grabbed the sponge, even though he was shivering, partly from having lost the body heat he had generated from paddling, and partly from sitting in four inches of cold lake water. It felt scary for him to lean over even a bit sideways to squeeze out the water-soaked sponge. But when a second, then a third wave crashed over the bow, he set about bailing in earnest. He knew that so much water in a canoe made it not only heavier, but tremendously unstable as the water sloshed about.

He bailed and bailed, then from behind him he heard his father whooping out loud and shouting, "Welcome to

Canada, Danny! We're having fun now!"

He shot a glance over his shoulder and could see that his father was actually smiling—paddling like a maniac and grinning like a fool. *My father really is crazy,* he thought to himself, soaked from the waist down, sitting in the bottom of a half-swamped canoe bobbing like a cork in the middle of a wind-ravaged lake a hundred feet deep. But no more giant waves crashed over the bow. The big sets were behind them.

An hour and a half later, they reached the lee shelter of the north shore of Lake Saganaga, a distance that on a calm day would have taken them only a half hour to cover. Hank steered them into a shallow bay and found a landing. Mike and Hank stepped out of the canoe into knee-deep water, then both men grabbed a shivering Danny, hoisted him out of the duffer's seat and stood him on shore.

"Move around," his father ordered. "You're nearly hypo-thermic."

Mike handed Danny one of Rosco's cinnamon rolls, slightly damp. "Eat. You need the calories."

Next, Mike and Hank quickly unloaded the canoe and emptied out the remaining water by each taking an end and turning the boat upside down. And just as efficiently, they loaded the packs back into the canoe.

"Get in." Hank motioned to Danny to get back into the bow seat. "It's the only way you're going to warm up enough to prevent hypothermia." But his frozen son couldn't seem to move, so he clinched Danny around the waist with one arm, lifted him up, waded again into the water and nearly threw him, like a little kid, into the canoe. Mike knew his place, and Hank again took the stern.

Danny soon realized that his father was right to put him back in the bow—as his body warmed with the exercise of paddling. And they had made it—across Sag in the wind—

across the big water. "How'd we do that?" Danny asked over his shoulder as they paddled close to shore, moving in a westerly direction toward the park, sheltered from the wind by towering stands of red pine, white pine and jack pine.

"The canoe knows what to do." He heard his father say. "Your grandfather was originally from Newfoundland. He knew something of the ocean, and he built that knowledge into the design of his White Otter canoes. That's why this canoe knows what to do in big water." Danny thought about this as he paddled.

From studying the map, he knew that the Quetico Provincial Park ranger station sat on an island about a half mile inside Cache Bay, a large bay that defined the northwesternmost section of Lake Saganaga. The entrance to Cache Bay itself passed through a narrows formed by two long points, like jaws forming a mouth. But what Danny hadn't realized, until they reached the narrows, was that the wind and waves out of the northwest were being funneled through that narrows—doubling their force. Up ahead, from the shelter of the lee shore, he could see huge whitecaps crossing from right to left in front of them. The passage to Cache Bay would not be easy.

Danny turned to look at his father. Mike turned his head, too. "Do you want us to switch places?" Danny was glad for Mike's offer.

"No! Danny and I can handle it." And with that, Danny could feel his father steering the canoe again into the wind. "Ten strokes, then switch." Danny nodded his head. Then, again without pause, they turned right into the open mouth of Cache Bay, wind and waves chewing down on them like rock-hard teeth.

SPLASH! SPLASH! SPLASH! Huge waves hit the bow, but none poured over the gunwales like out on the big lake.

Danny's arms and shoulders began to ache. *Sixty-five percent of the power.* Mike's words echoed in his head. He felt the same queasiness in his stomach that he felt when he got to the front of the line when it was his turn to do pull-ups in Phy. Ed. class. There, he knew he could just hang from the pull-up bar for a few seconds, then drop down, red-faced. Other kids couldn't do pull-ups either. But here, in the grip of Cache Bay's teeth, he was caught at the front of the line where he would have to prove himself to his brother and his father. But if he couldn't do even one pull-up, how could he provide sixty-five percent of the power from the bow?

"Come on, Danny, you can do it." It was Mike encouraging him from behind.

"...eight, nine, ten, switch!" his father yelled in the wind. Danny switched sides. He wanted to check his pockets, but he didn't dare stop paddling.

They hadn't moved an inch. He'd marked their progress against a bent cedar tree on the west point, and they hadn't moved an inch.

"Don't just use your arms," Mike coached. "Brace your legs and pull back with your whole torso."

The bow beneath Danny lifted clean out of the water just as he stroked down hard, sweeping only air with his paddle and nearly throwing himself over the left gunwale; but Mike, with his quick reflexes and long arms, grabbed him by the back of his PFD and pulled him back onto the bow seat.

"...eight, nine, ten, switch!" his father yelled again. Red-faced, Danny felt like crying in frustration and swearing at his dad. They had gained maybe a foot on his cedar tree marker. His arms and shoulders hurt now worse than ever.

Then, amazingly, the wind seemed to let up for just a few seconds, and with each stroke of the paddle the canoe surged forward and gained momentum. Momentum, that was the key—getting all that weight moving forward.

"...eight, nine, ten, switch!" With Mike coaching, he and his father found their rhythm for the optimum output and maximum effect. Canoeing, in that moment, had become for Danny a kind of physics experiment as well as a test of will.

He spotted the green roof of the ranger cabin on an island ahead of them. And as he paddled even harder, the pain left him and the joy filled him. They had done it! He had done it—broken through a wall of wind and waves and pain, and he had not given up!

The sign above the dock read: WELCOME to the QUETICO PROVINCIAL PARK. Danny was again relieved to arrive safely in a bay sheltered from the wind. He stepped up onto the wooden dock, a bit wobbly-legged, but he kneeled and steadied the canoe for Hank and Mike to climb out. The two men pulled all the packs and gear up onto the dock. They lifted the blue canoe out of the water as well and turned it over on the dock. Then they put their arms around Danny's shoulders, each holding an open hand out in front of him.

"What?" Danny asked.

"Snickers bars. We know you're packed heavy. One for my doing your sixty-five percent back there." Hank grinned.

"And one for my coaching." Mike smiled hungrily.

Danny unzipped his PFD and unbuttoned his left shirt pocket, producing the cherished candy bars. He gave one each to his brother and his father, and pulled the wrapper off the third for himself. "Thanks, guys. I guess this makes us even."

Mike leaned over to him. "You didn't think for a minute that we were going to let you bring any food into the tent, did you? Because, it's a well-known fact, Snickers bars are a black bear's favorite food."

Hank motioned for Danny to follow him up a steep trail

to the ranger station, while Mike stayed back to fix TL. It was about noon. Apparently no other canoeists had crossed Sag that morning. Ranger Molly O'Brien met them at the door to the ranger station—a log cabin. She and Danny's father had known each other for years, from the time Hank had guided trips for the youth camp.

"Good to see you, Hank. I saw your name on the permit reservation roster for today, and when I looked out at the narrows, I figured it must be you stuck out there. You're the only one I know fool enough to put this boy in the bow on a brutal day like this."

Danny couldn't tell if she was teasing his father, or was really on his case.

"Molly, this is my son, Danny. He did a great job out there and we made it just fine, thank you. Danny, this is Ranger Molly, an old friend who thankfully takes her job very seriously."

Ranger Molly handed Danny a cup of hot cocoa and his father a cup of coffee. "It's a good thing Maddy wasn't here to see this."

Hank didn't respond. He just sipped his coffee as Ranger Molly reviewed all the park rules, talking directly to Danny the whole time, making sure he understood about fire pits, personal latrines, no soap in the lake, no motors on most lakes and no feeding the bears. "And if you get in trouble and have to send someone for help, we won't send a plane unless you know exactly where you are on the map. There's over four thousand square kilometers of wilderness out there, and we're not going to chase all over the place looking for you."

Where's my GPS device? Danny thought to himself. *My cell phone?*

Hank told Ranger Molly that the threesome planned to head north into the park along the dangerous Falls Chain. She gave him another serious look as she handed him a detailed map of the water route through the series of nine waterfalls. The map indicated on which side of the channel to approach the portage around each of the falls. With its strong currents, the Falls Chain route was a challenging bit of paddling for even the most experienced of campers.

Hank paid the park fee and bought a fishing license. Danny also saw him stuff a twenty dollar bill into a jar marked *Friends of the Quetico.* Then he bought a Quetico sweatshirt each for Mike and Danny. Ranger Molly gave them their permit. "Have fun and be safe," she said to Hank. To Danny, Ranger Molly seemed to read his father rather well, with his inclination for taking risks.

As they turned to step out the door of the ranger cabin, Danny noticed a map of the Quetico on the wall. At different locations on the map someone had pinned up little paper cut-outs of black bears. "What are these?" he asked.

"Oh, those are the locations of nuisance bears—campsites where campers have reported problems. But, by this time of the season, these bears have probably moved on. They could be anywhere now."

Great, Danny thought to himself, *bears anywhere, bears everywhere.*

"Remember," Ranger Molly continued, "the park is here for the bears too."

Danny nodded his head, studying their route on the map for any bear cut-outs.

Back near the dock, Mike had set up trail lunch. Each sierra cup held an ounce of cheese, an ounce of salami, three pilot biscuits, a chunk of chocolate and a handful of gorp. A container of peanut butter sat open, and in a plastic water bottle he had mixed up a quart of bug juice—lemonade flavor. The three of them raised their cups for the traditional toast. "Foresters leave no trace," they said in unison.

Danny opened the big blade to his Swiss army knife and scooped out a glob of peanut butter, spreading it on his biscuits. The three of them ate steadily, their appetites and the need for quick energy both high, yet none wanting to wolf down his food without savoring each tasty morsel. They looked back over the lake from where they had come, white-caps still licking the air across the mouth to Cache Bay. Then they washed the last of their lunch down with lemonade and loaded up the canoe again.

Hank snapped a photo of his sons against a background of the ranger station sign with another maple leaf flag flapping in the wind. Danny took a moment to transfer his mini-first aid kit from his pants pocket to the shirt pocket that had held the Snickers bars. It was his turn to duff and Mike's turn to paddle bow. He wasn't sure if his father would ever paddle bow. He didn't know if his father always took the stern just to be in control, or if his weight in the front would make them too bow-heavy to maneuver the canoe.

As they paddled away from the ranger station island, Danny saw the first bank of dark clouds rolling in from the northwest. Soon it would be raining. Fortunately, they were sheltered from the worst of the wind as they headed for the portage around Silver Falls—Danny's first big Quetico portage. He hoped it didn't start raining until after they had crossed over it.

"Where's the portage, Dan-Man?" Another test from his father.

Danny scanned the horizon and the shoreline. His father had taught him to look for a low spot along the horizon, an opening in the trees, a slash mark on a tree trunk or a probable landing spot. Soon enough, at the far northwestern corner of a long narrow inlet, Danny could see the trees in the background moving in the opposite direction from the trees in the foreground—signifying a break in the forest where a channel of water flowed. And, beneath the wind, he could hear the low rumbling of Silver Falls. "There," he pointed, in the direction his father had already aimed the canoe.

The portage around Silver Falls was seven hundred meters, or one hundred forty rods as measured on the American side—nearly half a mile. Danny wondered what pack he would be asked to carry—the personal pack, the equipment pack or the crusher food pack? After crossing Sag, he felt like he had already battled wind and water, and worked harder physically than on any other day in his life. He hoped he still had enough reserves of energy left for whatever weight his father loaded onto his back.

Mike was first to step out into the water at the landing, then Hank, with Danny last—all three of them standing knee deep next to the canoe. It seemed again to Danny that his father and brother knew exactly what to do without even talking, just a series of grunts and nods. With that, Hank wrestled the food pack out of the stern compartment just as Mike backed into the straps. Then, to Danny's amazement, Hank threw the personal pack on top of the food pack as Mike pulled one of the straps down in front of his chest to steady the top pack. He was double-packed, and obviously thrived on the challenge of it as he flashed a big smile at his little brother.

Danny watched, still in amazement, as the Moose sloshed effortlessly through the water, stepped up onto the rocky portage path and disappeared into the woods almost at a run—the roar of Silver Falls much louder now, right at the portage.

"How's your footing?" his father asked.

"Good." Danny nodded.

"You take the equipment pack and the cook kit. When you get up on shore, wait for me to pass you with the canoe, then stay with me on the portage."

Danny accepted the weight of the equipment pack on his back, and grabbed the cook kit rope with his right hand, glad he wasn't carrying the food pack, or worse—double-packing. The equipment pack was heavy enough as he sloshed slowly out of the lake and up onto the rocky landing to wait for his father.

Next, Hank stowed the paddles, slipped his rucksack onto his back and centered himself alongside the yoke of the canoe, securing his footing beneath the water. Then, in an action that never ceased to impress Danny, his father flipped the canoe up onto his shoulders in a two-stroke movement. First he pulled the belly of the canoe up onto his thighs, bent like a table, then he thrust his gut out and threw the whole canoe up into the air, guiding it with his arms as the yoke pads landed squarely on his shoulders.

"It's all in the technique, doesn't take strength," his father would say, "but be sure not to move your feet."

Hank, too, sloshed out of the water like a moose, smiling at Danny. "I love to carry this beauty." He took off up the path into the forest. "Stay with me now," he called out. Danny followed.

Before long, Silver Falls appeared on their left, a magnificent cascade of white water dropping maybe a hundred feet through a narrow gorge between Lake Saganaga and Lake Saganagons. Hank stood at an opening in the trees overlooking the falls. From beneath his canoe, he was taking photos of the falls and of Danny with his pack.

"Here, take a picture of your father with a canoe on his back." He handed the camera to Danny, who had just caught up with him. His shoulders were pinched with pain and his legs were already aching. He was happy for the rest as he stepped back to snap a shot of his dad. Hank wore a big smile beneath his brimmed hat. He seemed oblivious to the fact that he was just standing around like a tourist, only with a hundred pounds of canoe on his shoulders, not to mention the rucksack. Danny couldn't understand how his sedentary, TV-watching, late-sleeping father had found the strength and energy to work this hard. *Mood swings?* Danny wondered.

Back on the portage trail at about the halfway point they came to a spot where a steep rock face, running up perhaps six feet, crossed the path, allowing for only a few toe holds. Here, portaging for Danny became like rock-climbing with a pack on his back, but his father never hesitated. He knew just where to step as he scaled the mini-cliff, stopping halfway up and reaching back with his hand. Danny grabbed it, joining his father beneath the canoe for a moment, and step for step, toe hold for toe hold, they overcame the obstacle.

From there the rocky, root-bare trail ran sharply up and

down. It was along this stretch that Danny began to pay the price for the soft life he had been leading—for all those hours of sitting in front of his computer screen or television, for all the nacho cheese dip and chips, pizza and pop, doughnuts and DQ's, and for not exercising. Maybe his brother was right; he should have gone to canoeing camp this summer.

The pack on his back felt as heavy as a boulder, and his body as weak as a leaf. A talon-like grip of pain had grabbed him by the back of his neck. He couldn't lift his head or even feel his arms and hands, both gone completely numb. He swore again under his breath, almost crying. But just as he was about to collapse onto the rocks, the trees ahead of him opened up, first to the sky, then to the lake below him; and he saw that he could make it, just barely, but he could make it.

Hank had already walked into the water and flipped his canoe down with a whoop. Mike worked frantically, loading the packs into the stern. And so, with his last reserves of energy, legs shaking, muscles aching, Danny staggered into the water, too—his father and his brother looking at him with wide grins across their faces.

"Welcome to the wall, little brother." Mike lifted the equipment pack off his shoulders. Hank secured the cook kit.

"Whadda' you mean?"

"I mean the wall you just hit." Mike laughed.

Then Hank and Mike grabbed Danny each by an arm and hoisted him into the duffer's compartment. He thought it was his turn to paddle bow, but he couldn't have even if he had wanted to; he couldn't even lift his arms.

Icy clouds had by now rolled completely overhead, blocking out the afternoon sun. No time to look back at Silver Falls, which stood behind them like a closed gate. The last outpost of civilization, the ranger station, stood one mean portage and a windy stretch of lake out of reach. No soft beds, no hot showers, no cold milk in the refrigerator for the next ten days. And as they moved out onto Lake Saganagons, the first big drops of rain plip-plopped towards them across the surface of the dark water. Sitting motionless and exhausted in the duffer's seat, Danny could feel the chill of the icy autumn rain already beginning to penetrate his bones.

His father and brother just seemed more energized by all this suffering. From behind him he could hear his father chuckling to himself and spewing forth with his own version of a Robert Service poem titled *Grin*:

> *"When your crusher pack is pinching and your arms are feeling numb—Grin.*
>
> *When your legs are feeling wobbly and from a bear you couldn't run—Grin.*
>
> *Don't let them know you're hurting, don't let them see you sweat,*
>
> *Though your back feels like it's breaking, and your feet are always wet;*
>
> *Push your body even harder, don't let the portage win the bet—And grin."*

Oh brother, Danny thought to himself, *what have I gotten myself into?*

chapter four

PORTAGING
THE FALLS

They had reached the campsite in a drenching downpour. Mike and Danny had scrambled to pitch the tent before the ground beneath it became too soaked. And by the time they had laid out the sleeping bags, Hank had a fire started—in the pouring rain! Danny had laughed at the sight of it. Wow! Was there anything his father could not do—drive all night without sleeping, paddle stern in wind and waves, portage pack and canoe, start a fire in the rain?

The sons helped their father stow the canoe up and away from the lake, resting it overturned on a soft patch of moss, with the paddles and life jackets tucked underneath. Mike tended to the leeches and nightcrawlers. Danny helped his father construct a tarp lean-to for the kitchen. Hank had packed the first night's dinner near the top of the food pack. And in short order, using a one-burner camp stove, he concocted his favorite Hudson Bay stew, pan-fried bannock and a pot of chocolate pudding for dessert.

Danny could not recall ever feeling as hungry in his life, or as thankful for a meal, as he felt on this night. Hank and Mike showed him how to break open the doughy bannock and pour the steaming red stew on top of the biscuits. There were no leftovers. Danny scraped the pudding pot clean as his last act before his father sent him into the tent. Exhausted, he changed into his sweat suit, crawled into his sleeping bag and fell asleep instantly, his new Quetico sweatshirt for a pillow. He had completely forgotten about going fishing.

In the morning, Danny awoke to the sounds of someone chopping wood and the pop and crackle of a wet-wood campfire. The smell of wood smoke drifted in through the mosquito-netting window of the red nylon tent. What time was it? How long had he been sleeping?

Lying there, against the hard ground, he added up his aches and pains, scrapes and bruises. It felt like every muscle, bone and joint in his body hurt. Stiffly, he sat up, pulled himself out from the warmth of his down sleeping bag and poked his head out the unzipped tent door, shivering in the cool air.

His father was standing by the fire, exactly where Danny had last seen him the night before. Mike was not far off, chopping wood with a steady crack-crack-crack of the ax. The heavy rain clouds from the day before seemed to have dropped down onto the forest floor during the night, turning the morning into a gray-white world of thick fog and chilling drizzle.

"Hey, camper." Hank spotted Danny. He walked toward him with the first aid kit in one hand and in the other,

Danny's socks and jeans, which he had dried over the fire. "Patch up any cuts and blisters, and put on these. Then get out here and help your brother carry wood. You gotta' earn your breakfast."

"Thanks." Danny grabbed his dry pants and socks. Looking up into his father's face he saw that a black stubble of whiskers had appeared, shading his already dark features; and his eyes looked bloodshot, more red than white—almost scary. Danny wondered if his father had slept at all during the night. But maybe the wood smoke had reddened his eyes. He sat back in the tent and opened the first aid kit, looking for moleskin and band-aids. After attending to his blisters, he pulled on the same pants and socks, stiff from being dried by the fire, he had worn the day before. Then he found his boots, never allowed inside the tent, always set just outside the tent. This was the worst part about wet-boot camping—in the morning, putting your warm dry socks and feet back into those cold wet boots.

The night before, he had carefully stashed all of his pocket survival gear in the stuff sack of his sleeping bag. Just as carefully he re-equipped himself, double-checking to make sure he hadn't lost anything: Swiss army knife, plastic whistle, waxed matches, flint and steel, mini-first aid kit, foil emergency blanket, flashlight, ten-in-one compass, fishing line and plastic leeches. It was all there except the Snickers bars. Then, kneeling just inside the tent with his boots sticking outside, he stuffed his sleeping bag, grabbed his hat and rain jacket and went to find Mike.

Back in the woods, safely away from the others, Mike had set up a chopping block, a six-foot length of a solid red pine log into which he had chopped a notch where he could set shorter lengths of wood upright to be split efficiently. He pulled off his safety goggles. "Hey, slacker. It's about time you got up." With an easy swing he stuck the ax head into the end of the chopping log. "Hold your arms out."

Danny held his arms out, palms up, as Mike loaded him up with split wood. He knew his older brother loved to chop wood when they camped, and he hoped he'd get a chance to chop wood, too; but for now, he'd have to settle for being a carrier of wood rather than a chopper of wood. He turned toward the campfire, arms aching with the weight of the wood piled nearly up to his chin, then he stopped and looked back over his shoulder. "Mike, did Dad go to sleep last night?"

Mike didn't look up from the pile of wood he was gathering for himself. "I don't know. Don't ask." He seemed irritated by Danny's question. "Just do your work. We've got a lot of ground to cover today."

Over by the fire, Danny dropped his armload of wood. His father handed him a sierra cup full of a lumpy, whitish gruel the likes of which Danny had never seen before. He looked at his dad. His dad smiled. "It's called rice and raisins. I only make it on the trail. It'll stick with you."

"Umm-umm." Mike joined them. "My favorite trail breakfast ever."

Danny tasted it, tentatively, then pretended to shudder. "Hey, not too bad." He was nearly as hungry as the night before, and gobbled up the sweet, cinnamon-flavored cereal, asking for seconds, then thirds. They drained a pot of cocoa. Hank quickly rinsed the dishes with boiled water from a third pot and assembled the cook kit. "Time to get going, Danny. We've got eight or nine portages between us and Kawnipi today."

Nine portages, geez. Just the thought of it made Danny's shoulders hurt.

Hank strapped down the food pack while Mike dropped

the tent. Danny doused the fire and cleaned out the fire pit. He shoveled a pile of wet ashes onto an ash tarp and buried the heap back in the forest away from the campsite, then rinsed the shovel and tarp with water from the lake. This was the order of things for now: his father—the tender of fires; his brother—the chopper of wood; and himself—the carrier of ashes.

Back at the fire pit Mike had neatly arranged a stack of firewood. Hank was squatted down in front of the fire pit itself, re-arranging the rocks and building a new fire for the next group of campers to light when they arrived at the campsite. Danny watched as his father assembled an assortment of small twigs, pine needles and thin strips of birch bark. Would it be teepee, log cabin or lean-to style? His father chose log cabin, and covered the delicate structure with a sheet of birch bark to protect against the rain.

"Okay, police the area. Leave no trace." Hank Forester was a fanatic about campsite clean-up. Not a speck of plastic, paper or foil would be left behind. He looked at Danny, his red eyes burning through the fog. "And remember, your father possesses special powers to spot campsite litter left behind by careless boys." Danny wasn't sure if his father was teasing, or if in that moment he actually believed he possessed special powers. He bent his head to the ground, pretending to look for litter, more worried about his sleep-deprived, red-eyed father than any scrap of plastic.

Danny was happy again to be back on the water and paddling bow, surrounded by the warmth and glow of the varnished cedar. In the gray of the morning, the wood seemed even more so to be the source of its own light. Mike duffed. Hank took the stern. It had stopped raining, but still a dense white fog covered the lake, totally obscuring the far shoreline. No wind. Quiet. The lonely cry of a single loon only added to the sense of eeriness and other-worldliness of paddling in fog.

"Should I shotgun?" Danny could see only a few feet in front of the blue canoe. He was worried about lake sharks and dead heads.

"No," his father answered, "I know this lake well enough."

But how, Danny wondered, as they headed in a northeast-erly direction, following for a long while the south shoreline barely visible on their right. Did his father's special powers include fog-vision?

Lake Saganagons stretched nearly twelve miles southwest to northeast—a maze of rugged islands, hidden bays and jagged shorelines. A long, irregularly shaped peninsula split the lake lengthwise down the center; but rather than paddle all the way around it, adding at least two hours of travel time, the threesome would take Dead Man's Portage traversing due north across the middle of the peninsula.

"Why do they call it Dead Man's Portage?" Danny broke a long silence.

"Because that's how you're gonna' feel after carrying the food pack over it," Mike quipped.

"No way, Moose." Danny splashed him with the blade of his paddle. "I bet it's because some old trapper died in a blizzard and they found his body on that portage."

"You're both wrong." Hank announced from the stern. "The peninsula is the dead man, the fossilized remains of the giant who pushed the glaciers back, then fell dead, face down in the lake. We'll walk across the small of his back." And with that said, Hank Forester turned the big blue eighteen-footer sharply to the left away from the south shoreline, due north, toward the giant's back, still engulfed in whiteness all around.

For Danny, paddling blind in the still whiteness of the

fog-shrouded lake felt almost as nerve-wracking as riding in the wind and waves on Lake Saganaga. He imagined the jagged edge of a rock, just below the black surface of the water, tearing open the bottom of the cherished boat—and him getting the blame. He wondered how his father knew to turn north just then with no landmark to give him his bearings. *Special powers?*

For another half hour he paddled rather gingerly through the mist, trying not to look like a lily-dipper. Then, out in front of him he was just able to see the twisted shapes of cedar trees along the shoreline. A great blue heron took flight from the shallows. And before long, straight ahead through the fog, his father delivered them, like some magic trick, to the portage landing.

Danny knew the routine. They all stepped out into the water, this time a mud bottom instead of gravel or rock. And this time, Mike double-packed the equipment pack with the personal pack, leaving the dreaded crusher pack for Danny. Mike hadn't been kidding.

"It's only sixty rods, less than half as long as yesterday." Hank lifted the beast out of the canoe and held it up for Danny to back into the straps. "Bend over slightly, try to carry the weight more with your legs than with your back." Danny sunk deeper into the mud, though the monster pack didn't feel quite as heavy as it had at home. "Swing your arms like a gorilla; and if you fall, turn sideways and let the pack land with its own weight. Don't try to break your fall with your arms, or you'll break both your wrists."

With the crusher pack on his back and the cook kit in his arms, Danny staggered out of the water and trudged slowly uphill between two huge white pine trees. *Sixty rods,* he calculated. *A rod is sixteen and a half feet—about the length of a canoe. Sixty canoe lengths. I can do that. I can do that,* he reassured himself.

At the top of the first climb, Hank whistled by him with his canoe and rucksack. "You're lookin' good, camper. Stay with me now."

Danny puffed out a breathless, "Okay." But his arms had already gone numb and his legs were aching. Still, he had made the first climb, and the trail ahead of him, though muddy from the rain, at least leveled out. He followed his dad, who had a little too obviously slowed down for him.

"Danny, look here!" His father sounded excited. Danny caught up to him standing alongside the path, canoe on his shoulders. "What do you see?"

Danny looked down at the fresh split hoof print in the mud. "Moose."

"Yes!" Hank took off, and fifty yards further down the trail he stopped again, his canoe still atop his shoulders. "Here," he called out to Danny.

And Danny caught up to him again, puffing, resting the weight of the food pack against a birch windfall.

"Look." Hank pointed down.

"What is it?"

"Wolf scat. Fresh. What does *that* tell you?"

"Moose and wolves in the area."

"Maybe right here last night!" Hank sounded intense, excited—still red-eyed.

And so they hiked, from hoof print to scat to feather to leaf; and Danny began to realize that for his father, a portage trail was really a Hank Forester nature trail, full of discoveries. And before he knew it, he was headed downhill to the north arm of the lake on the other side of the portage. His father was almost running, now, ahead of him into the water, flipping down with a whoop.

Mike grabbed the cook kit and pulled the crusher pack off

his back. "Hey, one-speed, I guess I'll have to give Coach Jones a good report." Danny smiled weakly, sweating, working to get the feeling back in his arms. Then Mike handed him a sierra cup and poured him a couple of glugs of freeze-dried orange juice from a water bottle.

Hank opened up his map case and spread the blue and white waterproof paper over the packs set in the canoe as they stood knee deep in the lake, drinking orange juice and looking at the map. Before them lay a route marked DANGEROUS WATERS—the Falls Chain. They looked out at the lake, still white with fog. Hank set his compass on the stern seat for a fresh reading. "Come on," he said, "if we want to make it to Kawnipi and still have time to fish before dark, we gotta' push on."

They were careful to wash the mud from their boots before climbing back into the canoe. Danny duffed and Mike took the bow. And once again they were afloat, this time headed towards dangerous waters, surging rapids and churning falls—with about fifty feet of visibility.

Why don't we just wait until the fog lifts, Danny thought to himself. But he didn't dare question his sleep-deprived, red-eyed, push-tripping father. Instead, he double-checked his pockets and tightened his PFD. Besides, according to the map, they wouldn't reach the first set of falls for at least another hour. Maybe they'd get lost on the way.

The route to the Falls Chain turned them back in a north-westerly direction. Again, they fell silent, following the faint shoreline, working their way past ghost-like islands, muted colors and muffled sounds all around. Not even the chattering of squirrels could be heard. Occasionally, Hank would call out for Mike to stop paddling. From behind him, Danny could hear his father working with map and compass. Then he would signal for Mike to start again, making a slight adjustment in their course. Finally, even Danny realized that they had entered a channel of fast moving water.

"Shhh..." Hank whispered.

Mike held still, resting his paddle across his lap. The canoe moved forward by itself, pulled by the current. Carefully they listened; and then, ahead of them in the fog, they could hear the distinctive low rumble of a waterfalls.

"The portage is on the left, very near the lip of the falls. You know what to do."

Mike nodded his head.

"Danny, if we dump and end up going over the falls, which we will not, but if we do, keep your feet pointed downstream in the rapids and stay upstream of the canoe."

Danny nodded his head too, and cinched his PFD to maximum tightness. He imagined one of those scenes from a Disney wilderness movie where the canoe breaks in half and the kid tumbles for miles down the rapids, then spends weeks fighting his way back to civilization, living off of tree bark and slugs.

Fifty feet. They would have about fifty feet of visibility, three canoe lengths, to spot the portage and land safely above the falls. The current had already picked up speed, pulling them faster and faster. They hugged the left shoreline, rocks and trees flying by now.

"There! There!" Hank shouted.

"I got it! I got it!" Mike shouted back over the roar of the falls.

"Back paddle! Back paddle! Scull!"

Danny's heart raced as his father and brother back paddled furiously against the swift current and then deftly sculled the boat sideways into the landing. Mike sprang out of his seat and planted his feet solidly on the rock shelf, never letting go of the left gunwale. Hank stepped out quickly as well, onto the rock landing, like a natural dock. The two men held the floating canoe in place with a smiling Danny, sitting like a prince in the duffer's seat.

"Should we let him go?" Mike awaited instructions from the king.

"No, the canoe's too valuable."

"Jerks!" Danny protested. But when he stepped onto the landing, his father hung the personal pack on his back. Then he threw his rucksack on top of the personal pack.

"There, you can tell Coach Jones you double-packed. Now get going. We'll catch up with you."

Thankful for the light load, Danny grabbed the cook kit, took off down the portage trail—and entered yet another world. Already, there had been the world of wind and waves on big Sag, and the world of gray-white silence on giant Saganagons. But suddenly, here, at this place called Four Falls, the fog had disappeared completely. Around each bend of the open portage trail, whole new vistas appeared. Splashes of red maple and yellow aspen stood against a brilliant blue sky. Tremendous surges of blue-green water poured over bare rock outcroppings. Each falls dropped just two or three meters, then rolled into whitewater rapids before spilling over the next falls. All of this motion seemed to propel Danny headlong down the portage path. He barely noticed the weight he was carrying.

Hank and Mike blew past him about halfway, shouting in their excitement at the falls, Hank with the equipment pack and canoe, Mike with the food pack. At the end of eighty rods, they put in again and paddled a short distance to the fourth falls for a quick ten rod portage. Then Hank let Danny paddle bow as they crossed over to the other side of the channel, cutting across the swift current to the short portage around Bald Rock Falls. Here, in the bright mid-day sun, they stopped for TL, sitting on a smooth, flat, exposed patch of granite just a few feet from the roaring water.

Hank laid back on the sun-warmed rocks, looking up at the sky. "Imagine being here, at this spot, eleven thousand years ago, at the end of the last ice age, with a mile high glacier crushing down on you. That's what shaped this whole region, the grinding movement of glaciers. If you could have been up in a space shuttle looking down on Earth when the glaciers first receded, you would have seen this vast expanse of exposed bedrock we now call the Canadian Shield. The waters melting from the glaciers formed all of these lakes and rivers."

Danny bit into one of his mother's voyageur bars, sipped his cherry-flavored bug juice and tried to imagine a mile of ice above his head.

"First came the lichens, then the mosses and scrub brush. Blueberries are actually one of the oldest plants around. Eventually the big trees took root. Too bad the woolly mammoths and sabretooth tigers are gone. They would have made this a real interesting trip." Hank sat up. "Time to go."

Danny paddled bow again for the next stretch, an hour or so cutting across the east end of Wet Lake to Little Falls and a beauty of a portage—a pine needle path high above the falls, so pretty it was hard to leave. But Kawnipi called, and the meanest work of the day lay ahead.

At Koko Falls the team reverted to their original pack assignments. Mike double-packed the food and personal packs. Danny took the equipment pack and cook kit. Hank, the canoe and rucksack. As Danny waited for his dad to flip up the canoe, he set the cook kit on a tree stump and picked up a long, thin beaver-chew—a white aspen stick about six feet long with all the bark chewed off of it. Somehow it had floated to the portage landing, though Danny hadn't noticed any beaver lodges along the way.

He watched his father. This time Hank seemed to struggle a bit with flipping up the old White Otter canoe. And this time the portage didn't run so openly and easily downhill along the rushing waters. Instead, the trail twisted steeply back up into the forest. Before they were finished, sixty rods would seem like a hundred—up and down, rocks and roots, windfalls and muskeg. Finally the trail broke steeply back downhill into a rocky gorge, past a moss-covered cliff to a poor landing below the falls, so tight there was barely enough room to flip the canoe down.

Danny poked along with the aid of his new beaver-chew walking stick, his muscles pinched and aching again, nearly falling at times. As he made his way down through the gorge, he could see his father and brother standing in the water by the canoe beneath the branches of a cedar tree, patiently waiting for him, the canoe all loaded up except for the equipment pack. When he reached them, Mike stepped forward and pulled the pack off his back. What a relief. Then his red-eyed, unshaven father looked at him rather grimly, directly into his eyes. "Where's the cook kit?" he asked.

Oh, no, Danny felt suddenly sick to his stomach. *What have I done?* And he realized that when he picked up the beaver-chew, he had forgotten the cook kit sitting on the tree stump back at the beginning of the portage.

"Go get it," his father ordered.

Danny could not recall his father's voice ever sounding more angry with him, or more disappointed. He turned without looking and started back, throwing his prized stick down on the rocks beside the trail. From behind him he could hear Mike protesting to his father. "Come on, Dad, it'll take Danny an hour. Let me run back."

"No," his father said. And that was final.

But what about always sticking together on portages? Danny recalled his mother's instructions. He didn't like the idea of going off on his own. And, as he walked, what really bothered him was the thought of bears. Back in the forest the upturned root wads of wind-fallen trees resembled the dark shapes of bears. But what if one of those dark shapes really turned out to be a bear? What if a bear found him alone in the woods? He felt for his plastic whistle and tried to hurry, but the climb back up the gorge trail and the hike along the rugged portage was almost as difficult without a pack on his back.

Finally, though, he made it back to the beginning of the portage; and thankfully, the treasured cook kit was sitting right where he had left it. He gripped the canvas bag tightly, turned around and jumped with a startle. There, just a few yards up the trail, stood his father. Neither said anything to the other, they just turned and headed back again over the brutal portage. Danny followed, carrying the cook kit.

"Dad," he finally spoke up, about halfway across, "how do you make this portaging look so easy? It just about kills me."

"You gotta' use your imagination, Danny." Hank put his arm around his son's shoulder and took the cook kit from him. "For instance, when I'm bogged down up to my waist in muskeg on a swampy portage, I pretend I'm a bull moose. If I find an open trail, maybe across a high, rocky area, I try to run like a wolf. Once in a while I'll really get going downhill, almost flying like an eagle. But on a portage like this one, tough going, rocky, up hill and down, I imagine I'm a big black bear. That's why I growled at you at the end of the portage—I was still in my bear mind. I'm sorry."

"I'm sorry too," said Danny, "for messing up."

They walked a little farther.

"Do you see those downed trees over there, where the roots pull up the ground?" Hank pointed to the windfalls in the forest. "From a distance, where the black dirt shows, I always think I'm seeing the silhouette of a bear in the woods. It kinda' scares me sometimes."

"Ya, I know what you mean." Danny had never considered that his father might be afraid of bears, too. No, it couldn't be.

Mike was waiting for them, studying the map. Hank picked up Danny's beaver-chew stick and examined it. "This isn't a beaver-chew, Danny. These are the teeth marks of a Maymaygwayshi."

"What?"

"Maymaygwayshi—an Ojibwe trickster, a little guy who can disappear into the crevases between rocks. He pulled a trick on you by placing this stick in your path, diverting your attention away from the cook kit." Hank broke the stick over his knee and threw the pieces far back in the woods. Danny shook his head. *Why would a Maymaygwayshi want to pull a trick on me?* he wondered as he climbed back into the canoe.

The channel at Canyon Falls split around a high, wedge-shaped rock of an island, creating the longest drop and the fastest moving, most powerful, most dangerous waterfalls of all. Danny struggled again with the crusher food pack, fifty rods, this time not forgetting the cook kit. But along the way, he marveled at the clusters of cedar trees and the incredibly deep carpet of yellow-green moss on either side of the trail, whose thick growth had been promoted by the constant mist rising above the churning waterfalls.

A quick hike around Kennebas Falls, their eighth and final portage of the day, delivered them, trail worn and weary, to magnificent Kawnipi Lake, deep in the Quetico wilderness. With its sweeps of yellow-leafed birch against the vast dark pine forest, the great lake welcomed them to autumn up north. And then, for nearly two more hours, Hank and Mike paddled steadily into a light afternoon breeze until they finally reached their destination—a place Danny's father called Eagles' Nest Island, in the very heart of Kawnipi.

A huge pile of split firewood greeted them at the open, flat-rock campsite, so Danny and Mike were free to go fishing while Hank made dinner. They fished from shore for small-mouth bass. No luck. But Hank had cooked up a pot of chili-mac, with cornbread and brownies baked in a reflector oven set in front of the open fire. They gorged themselves, slathering their cornbread with butter and honey.

After the dishes were washed and the tent was pitched and the packs were stowed, they sat out beneath the stars, tending to a stump fire, sipping cocoa. When the cocoa pot emptied, Hank set his insulated, stainless steel trail cup down on a rock, then walked to the water's edge. There, he cupped his hands in front of this mouth and let out with a long, loud, wolf-like howl, which he repeated several times. Danny and Mike joined their father in the howling. Then they listened, intently. And soon enough, from across a distant ridge, came the distinct sound of a lone wolf howling, greeting them in the night.

chapter five

KAWNIPI LAYOVER

Bacon. The smell of frying bacon wafted in through the open tent door. For a second night, Danny had been the first to fall asleep and the last to wake up in the morning. He and Mike had crawled into the tent after the fire had died down and the wolf-men had stopped howling. Hank had stayed up to stir the coals until they turned to ash. So again, Danny wasn't sure if his father had slept at all that night.

Mike reached into the tent, grabbed Danny's toe and pulled it hard. "Come on, little brother, the fish aren't going to wait." He was right. Best to get out on the water early, before the sun climbed too high. Danny scrambled to dress, re-equip himself with his pocket survival gear and find his boots. Then he met Mike and his father near the fire pit.

Layover day—no paddling or portaging, and they would eat big, just like at Rosco's place. Hank had cooked half the bacon, a mess of hash browns and a huge stack of buttermilk pancakes. He was stirring pure maple syrup granules into a small pot of boiling water just as Danny reached the kitchen.

Mike was mixing another bottle full of freeze-dried orange juice.

"I'm starved," Danny announced. "That rice and raisins didn't stick with me as long as you said it would." He thought he was looking thinner, less pudgy, and he could feel that his muscles were tighter.

"Well, this ought to do it." Hank handed him a plate heaped with pancakes. Danny noticed that his father's whiskers had grown even heavier, and his eyes seemed more dark now, than red. "Nothing to do today but eat and fish and sleep, and then eat and fish and sleep some more." Danny hoped his father would get some sleep.

Hank inhaled deeply. "What a great day to be in the Quetico."

And a glorious fall day it promised to be—clear blue sky and sky-blue water already smooth as glass. Not a bug in sight, and the only sign of other human beings was a thin wisp of smoke rising above the trees from a distant campsite across the lake. Fall fishing promised to be nearly at its best, only better if it was raining; but Danny would take the warm sun and dry skies today.

"I've got us all ready to go." Mike hurried Danny along. He had already tied the floating canoe up to a cedar branch hanging out over the lake.

"You guys go out for now. I'll try my luck later." Hank motioned for Danny not to forget his life jacket. "When you get back, I'll have some doughnuts for you."

Mike had fashioned a makeshift anchor by tying the end of a rope to a large rock, which he set on his life jacket in the canoe so as not to scratch the varnished wood. He stuck

Danny's rod and reel in the bow compartment along with his paddle. Danny stepped into the canoe off of a flat rock sticking out of the water, and they pushed off, planning to circle the big island.

Before trying their leeches and nightcrawlers, Mike suggested spinners and shads. They drifted counter-clockwise around the island, casting toward shore, no strikes. Then, on the far side of the island they found a shaded bay and dropped anchor near where a jack pine windfall angled into the water. There, they switched to live bait.

Mike set up a bobber-stopper for Danny, putting his leech about a foot off the bottom in twelve feet of water. Then he hooked up a nightcrawler for himself. Their stick-like fluorescent-orange slip-bobbers stood almost perfectly still in the water on either side of the canoe. "Let 'em take it now, Danny. Let 'em run with it before you set the hook. I know they're down there." Danny waited patiently, staring intently at his bobber.

"Did you bring the landing net?"

"Yes. That's what I like to hear—confidence." Mike pushed the release button on the handle of the collapsible landing net and the whole apparatus popped open with a snap. "I've got the stringer, too."

"Good."

Then, soon enough, Danny's bobber disappeared with a quick dart beneath the surface of the water. "I got one!" He whispered loudly to Mike. "I got one."

"Let him take it. Let him take it. I know it's a walleye." Mike coached.

"Now!" he yelled. "Set the hook!"

Danny pulled back hard on his rod and could feel the weight of a great fish on the end of his line. "I got him! I got him!" He reeled and pulled, reeled and pulled, his thin fishing line zigzagging back and forth through the water.

"I got the net." Mike kneeled forward in the stern compartment and leaned his body toward Danny, net in hand. "Play him out, little brother, play him out."

But just when Danny should have let out the line, he pulled back way too hard. His rod tip snapped up straight and his hook, minus the great fish, flew out of the water, ripped through the air and embedded itself deeply into Mike's lower lip.

"Ow! Ow! Ow!" Mike threw down the net and grabbed Danny's fishing line, blood running down his chin. "I can't believe you did that, you little..." and mumbled something Danny couldn't hear. Then he cut the fishing line with his fillet knife, reeled in his nightcrawler and pulled up the anchor. "Paddle!" he shouted as best he could with a fish-hook in his lip. Danny kept silent. He didn't dare look back at Mike. He had never paddled harder.

Back at the campsite Hank met them knee deep in the water, keeping the White Otter off the rocks. "Go sit down by the fire. I'll be right there." Then he flipped up the canoe and carried it up into the campsite, setting it down behind the tent.

"Lemme' see it." Hank opened the first aid kit and pulled Mike's hand away from his mouth. Danny watched. Mike glared at him. "The barb is all the way in, buried. What do you want me to do? I can try to pull it back out, or I can push it all the way through and clip off the barb."

"Push it through," Mike mumbled, his lip beginning to swell, "but I want Danny to do it. He's the first aid expert on this trip, the future physician."

Hank looked at Danny. Danny shrugged his shoulders. "Okay," he said, "but I've never really done this before." Hank handed him the small needle-nosed pliers from the first aid kit. Danny studied his fishhook up close. "Ready?" he asked. Mike nodded. Then, Danny gripped the hook with the pliers and, with a quick twist of his wrist, he drove the barbed end out through Mike's lip.

"Ouch," Mike winced.

"I can't decide if you look like a northern pike, a walleye or a smallmouth," Hank smiled at Mike. Mike growled.

Then, just as deftly, Danny clipped the barb off with the wire cutter and pulled the shaft of the hook, with a length of fishing line still tied to it, back out through Mike's lip. "Sorry, Mike," he said, handing his brother a medicated band-aid.

"Forget it. I shouldn't have had my face sticking out into your casting zone."

"That was a mighty fine demonstration of wilderness first aid, young man." Hank seemed especially proud of his son, and seemed to have forgotten about who had sunk the hook into Mike's lip in the first place.

"Mom says I have the hands of a surgeon."

"Indeed. Well, your mother knows a natural born healer when she sees one." Hank closed up the first aid kit. "I'd say this calls for some doughnuts. I'll get my dough ready. You guys round up some firewood." He turned to the food pack.

Mike grabbed the red-handled ax and safety goggles. He handed Danny the bow saw, and the two brothers headed back into the woods away from the campsite.

In the spirit of *leave no trace,* Danny had learned another one of his father's rules—no firewood could be gathered from within a two hundred foot radius of the fire pit. So Danny and Mike followed a trail into the interior of the island where they found all the downed and dead firewood they would need, and Mike even showed Danny how to pull pine knots out of logs, especially red pine, rotting on the forest floor.

But Danny wanted to chop wood, so Mike set up a chop-

ping block, and together they took turns sawing foot and a
half lengths of dry logs, about four inches in diameter. Mike
showed Danny how to split thin sticks of wood for a baking
fire—the more surface area of wood, the hotter the fire in
front of the reflector oven. Then for an hour or more Danny
chopped wood, at first missing his target more often than
not, but eventually getting the hang of it.

"Don't swing so hard with your arms," Mike coached.
"Bend your knees and just let the ax head drop with its own
weight and the weight of your body dropping down. Just
kinda' guide the ax with your arms." Danny focused his aim
on the next length of wood, centering the blade as he
dropped the ax again. CRACK! The wood exploded as split
wood will, clean and white on the inside. He had become a
chopper of wood, and he had worked up a woodchopper's
sweat and appetite.

They dumped their armloads of wood near the fire pit,
and changed out of their trail boots into their campsite
shoes—old sneakers. Boots were for portaging, paddling,
chopping wood and swimming.

Hank was over by the canoe, rolling out his doughnut
batter on its wide blue belly. Danny remembered his father's
motto: water, air and bread dough. With the cover from the
freeze-dried orange juice and the cap from the vegetable oil,
he was cutting out his trail doughnuts. A pan of oil sizzled on
the camp stove. A mixture of sugar and cinnamon sat piled
high on a plate next to the stove. He had already shaken up a
fresh bottle of bug juice.

"Hey, Danny," his father quizzed him, "in what country
were doughnuts first made?"

"I dunno'."

"In Greece." Hank smiled. Danny groaned.

The first doughnut landed in the hot oil, bubbled up and

floated to the top. Perfection. Soon there were a dozen sugared doughnuts and a dozen doughnut holes to share between them. Doughnuts and bug juice—no need for the traditional trail lunch on layover day.

After they had scarfed up every last crumb, Hank pulled a thick climbing rope out of the equipment pack. "Nap time," he said, then walked toward the huge white pine that stood alone and apart from all the other trees in the open, flat-rock campsite. Mike followed with a rock-climbing harness he had pulled out of the equipment pack. Danny wondered what was going on. Mike waved him over to the big tree.

Typically, the great white pines in the northern forests can grow as tall as one hundred and twenty feet. And typically, standing together, they lose their lower branches all the way up to the top twenty feet or so, making it nearly impossible to climb these giant trees. But occasionally, a lone white pine will take root in an open area of the forest, perhaps near the shore of a lake or on an island. In this environment, the tree may hang onto its lower branches, perhaps as low as eight or ten feet above the ground, making it a perfect tree for climbing. Such was the case with the exceptional white pine tree standing alone on Eagles' Nest Island.

Danny and Mike met up with their father at the base of the tree. Danny now understood what was up. "Hey, I don't know about this. Are you guys sure this is a good idea?" *Mom didn't say anything about climbing trees,* he thought to himself. *She probably never dreamed of something like this.* He looked up apprehensively at the branches.

"You'll be totally safe," Mike tried to reassure him. "I brought this along." He held up his climbing harness. "We use these all the time fighting fires out west."

Danny stepped into the leg holes of the harness. Mike strapped him in tight, clipped on two carabiners and tied one end of the rope to the carabiners.

Then Hank boosted Mike up onto the lowest branch. Mike pulled up Hank, and together they pulled Danny up into the lower branches of the tree. From there, climbing up the open branch structure of the white pine was as easy as climbing a ladder. Still, Danny was shaking inside the whole way to the top.

At about eighty feet above the rocky ground they stopped, each taking up a separate position on a branch, with their backs against the trunk of the tree. Hank and Mike had kept a tight grip on Danny and his rope all the way up, and now they took turns lashing Danny and each other to the tree so they wouldn't fall out. A light breeze blew from the southeast, swaying the branches, gently rocking the visitors.

Danny surveyed the island. "Where's the eagles' nest?" he asked.

"This is the eagles' nest," Hank motioned to the tangle of branches and rope holding them secure, "and we are the eagles." He smiled a tired-looking smile at Danny.

"Dad's the only one who calls this Eagles' Nest Island," Mike explained. "There's no real eagles' nest here."

Danny felt certain he understood. *Now I know my father is crazy,* he thought to himself. Looking over at his dad, he saw that he had already fallen asleep, swaying like a baby in the arms of the giant whispering pine, his head resting in the elbow-like crook of a branch, the long soft pine needles, like fingers, stroking his face. It was the first time in four days that Danny had actually seen his father sleeping.

Mike put his finger to his lips to keep Danny quiet, then he pointed up into the sky high above the tree line to the north. There, soaring on the updrafts of the afternoon wind, two magnificent bald eagles drifted eastward, crisscrossing through the air, their wings spread wide. Danny watched them for a long while. He had stopped shaking inside, but he could not fall asleep, so he tried to take in as much of the lake as he could. His father had told him he could try his hand at guiding. Maybe tomorrow. Kawnipi's six deep bays stretched for miles, spread out like eagles' wings extending from the main body of the lake. Toward the west, Danny spotted two silver canoes off in the distance, sunlight glinting off the paddles.

An hour later Hank Forester popped open his eyes. "I am restored," he announced. "Let's go fishing, and I'll show you boys how to catch the big one." Mike touched the swollen wound on his lip. Danny felt relieved to have his father back. It took them another hour to untie themselves, climb back down to the ground and load up the canoe for fishing.

Back at the jack pine walleye hole all three fished off the bottom with slip-bobbers and leeches, betting on Danny's earlier luck. For an hour or more they waited. Hank had them move into twenty feet of water. Then all of a sudden the fish hit hard and fast. First Mike landed a two-pound walleye, then Hank a three-pounder, then Mike another two-pounder. But Danny's bobber floated motionless.

"Check your bait," Hank suggested.

Danny reeled in his line. Sure enough, he'd lost his leech without even knowing it. "Gimme' a worm."

Mike handed him a carton of nightcrawlers. Danny dug through the tangled mess and pulled out the biggest, fattest nightcrawler he had ever seen, and he made sure he hooked it through its dark collar. Then he cast it over the side of the boat, but before his slip-bobber even hit the bobber-stopper he felt the great fish hit his bait. "Here we go again." Danny set the hook without being coached. His rod bent nearly double, so he reset the drag on his reel and let some line out.

"Play him, Danny, play him."

"I know. I know." The big fish was trying to run straight away. Danny pulled back steadily.

"I got the net. Just get him up by me." Mike sounded even more excited than Danny.

Danny played the fish, his heart racing the whole time, five-ten-fifteen minutes, gradually pulling the old fish in toward the canoe until Mike caught a glimpse of it just below the surface off the bow. "Oh, little brother, you have done it now! That is one awesome walleye!"

"He's not in the boat yet," Danny still feared losing it. "Watch out for flying hooks."

But quick as lightning Mike scooped the net into the lake and hauled out Danny's great fish—a ten-pound walleye! He dumped it into the bottom of the canoe next to Danny where it flopped hard against the wooden ribs. Wow! Danny tried to hold it down and take the hook out of its mouth.

"Let me do it." Hank leaned forward from the stern seat, smiling at Danny and shaking his head. "This is unbelievable. I've never seen a fish this big in my life." He was wearing the fire pit gloves he used to tend the fire, and grabbed the golden-colored fish by its lower jaw. Then he pulled Danny's fishhook away from the lower jaw of the fish with a long hook-remover out of the tackle box.

"What should we do with him?" Danny asked. The fish again whacked it's tail against the bottom of the canoe.

"It's your decision, Danny. Catch and release—or fillet and fry. But you must decide right now if you want him to go back in the water."

"Take a picture." Danny kneeled in the bottom of the canoe and lifted his thirty-inch prize up as high as he could reach for his father to snap a photo—proof that he had really caught such a fish. Then he leaned over the side of the canoe and gently set the exhausted fish back in the water. At first it didn't seem to want to move, so Danny rocked it back and forth pumping water through its gills, and soon enough, with a quick whip of its tail, it shot out of sight and headed for the dark seclusion of the deep water.

"Good man." Mike patted Danny on the back. "I gotta say, this takes the sting out of that hook in my lip." He too shook his head in disbelief.

After that, the three fishermen pulled in their lines and headed back around the island, the stringer of smaller walleyes trailing in the water alongside the canoe. Danny duffed. As Hank and Mike paddled, his father composed another rendition of a Robert Service poem:

"There are fish below in the Quetico, and many a man has

> *tried,*
> *But only one, a young son-of-a-gun, has landed the biggest*
> *walleye.*
> *His name was Dan, some called him Dan-Man, and his*
> *talents were widely known.*
> *No, he couldn't be topped and he couldn't be stopped, from*
> *bringing the biggest fish home."*

Danny beamed with pride listening to his father's corny poem. Sitting in the hold of the golden-wood canoe, he felt like a king being transported in his personal vessel across the royal waters.

Back at the campsite Mike skillfully filleted the three smaller fish they had caught, setting the fish guts, skins, heads and tails out on shoreline rocks for the night scavengers—weasels or mink.

"What about bears?" Danny asked.

"Not to worry," Mike reassured him, "not here, no signs of bear on this island."

Danny had to take him at his word, but he still didn't like the idea of leaving fish heads out on the rocks. He had heard about bears swimming to islands. But Hank Forester's fabulous fish fillet dinner took his mind off of this worry. The master trail chef had fried up the six fillets in a cornmeal batter, cooked a pot of potatoes au gratin and a pot of buttered corn; and he had even baked a yellow cake with chocolate frosting.

"Food for the gods, that's what walleye is, food for the gods." Hank called his sons to dinner. "We are like little gods in God's country."

They stood as they cut into the tender white fillets on their plates—heads nodding, moans of satisfaction all around. "Amen," they said in unison. "Amen."

"The taste of walleye is indescribable to me." Danny had

never eaten this much fish in his life.

"How you ever caught that fish is indescribable." Mike was still shaking his head in disbelief.

Danny smiled to himself, feeling a kind of warm glow inside. He knew he still had a lot to learn on the trail. He knew how to paddle bow, portage packs, pitch a tent and chop wood. Maybe tomorrow he would have a chance to guide with map and compass. Next year he could learn to paddle stern and bake with a reflector oven. Some day, he might even be able to carry a canoe or start a fire in the rain. But on this day, he had earned the respect and admiration, perhaps even the envy, of his father and his brother. He had done one thing better than either of them—he had caught the biggest fish—and on the trail, that counted for something.

Later, after dark, Hank cooked up another pot of cocoa and a bag of popcorn. Mike showed Danny how to burn pine knots in the fire, and the three of them sat for a long time watching the multicolored flames, each telling their part of the great fish story, now practically a legend.

When the fire died down they found their way to the open area of flat rock near the water's edge. There, they laid down with their backs against the granite still warm from the sun, and looked up at the night sky. The stars shone brighter than ever this night—all the constellations of the north. And then, unexpectedly, as they lay there, from every corner of Kawnipi, from every near and distant bay, arose the song of loons crying out in unison—filling the air with a rare kind of music, a symphony of natural sound sweeping back and forth across the waters for an hour or more. No one spoke. Finally, though, when the loons had quieted down, Danny sat up, feeling a bit chilly. Mike was awake; but their father had fallen into a deep sleep on the bedrock beneath the stars. He breathed heavily.

"I've seen this before," Mike said to Danny. "Wait here." He turned on his flashlight and walked over to the tent. In a minute he returned with their father's old sleeping bag in one hand and life jacket in the other. He put the life jacket under Hank's head, and covered him with the sleeping bag. "There's nothing else we can do."

Danny followed Mike back into the tent, thinking about his father asleep on the rocks beneath the stars, beneath the lone white pine, beneath the call of the loons. But when he crawled into his sleeping bag, laid his head down and closed his eyes, all he could see in his mind was the image of that great golden walleye swimming back and forth in the water.

chapter six

MOOSE CHASE

D anny and Mike both slept in late. By the time they crawled out of the tent Hank had fried up the last of the bacon and eggs. He had even baked a pan of caramel rolls. No telling when he had gotten up. Sleeping on the rocks like an animal hadn't seemed to bother him. On the ground next to the fire pit he had spread out the map of Lake Kawnipi, a rock holding down each corner of the waterproof paper.

"Danny, I want you to be our guide for today." Hank handed Danny his compass and map case.

The three campers studied their route on the map as they ate their breakfast. One of Danny's favorite winter activities was poring over wilderness maps with his dad. Hank had a whole stack of Quetico and Boundary Waters maps, and once in a while he would spread them out on the kitchen table late at night. They would trace over all the routes he had traveled as a guide for the youth camp. Together they would dream up new routes into the most remote lakes they could find.

"Remember," Hank poured himself a cup of coffee as he instructed his second son, "always turn your map in the direction of travel. Line up north on your compass with the north directional lines on your map."

"Where are we now?" Danny asked.

"Right here." Hank pointed to the island campsite. "And we want to go here." He drew his finger across the map to the very northwesternmost corner of Kawnipi where the lake pinched together in a maze of narrows and islands. "We'll camp somewhere around here tonight. Tomorrow we'll head south into Kahshahpiwi."

Danny concentrated on the map. Guiding on this day would challenge all of his map and compass skills, but he felt up to the task. Next to first aid, orienteering was his best trail subject. Besides, they would have the wind at their backs. An unusual southeasterly breeze, warm and humid, had continued blowing from the day before throughout the night. By mid-morning it felt almost hot. Shorts and T-shirts weather.

The voyageurs took their time breaking camp and carefully re-packing. The crusher food pack, with all the baking Hank had accomplished, had lost considerable weight. It was no longer the monster it had started out to be. The tent was dry and light.

Danny stacked firewood for the next group. Mike re-assembled the fire pit rocks, washing them off with water and setting the flattest rocks into the dirt, like a hearth, ideal for the placement of a reflector oven. The three of them rearranged eight bench-like logs in a circle around the fire pit. Then they stood back and admired their work. Perfect.

So it was almost noon by the time they set off, a bright

sun high in the sky to the south, a warm wind at their back. They would spend the rest of the day on the water, maybe just one portage, depending on how far they traveled. Mike even rigged up a lake trout spinner and set his rod and reel in front of him in the bow. Danny knelt in the duffer's compartment. He had folded the map and placed it in the clear plastic map case, zippered shut. The compass was attached by a lanyard to a grommet at the corner of the map case. Around his neck hung a small pair of binoculars that his father had taken out of his rucksack. His father had also set a bottle of grape bug juice and a plastic bag containing their trail lunch for the day in the duffer's compartment next to Danny. He would be the cook for lunch.

"Guiding from a map is a lot like painting a picture." Hank talked to Danny in his teaching voice as he paddled. "In painting you have to look at your subject, and then at your canvas, back and forth to capture the image you want. In guiding it's the same thing. You have to look up at the points and bays and islands you can see out in front of you, then down at your map. In your mind you have to adjust the features of the landscape to the scale of your map in order to understand where you are on the map."

Danny pointed to a gap between a point and an island. "There," he directed his father.

"Okay, trail guide Dan." Hank and Mike dipped their paddles in unison. Great Kawnipi spread out in all directions. Fall colors everywhere.

An hour or so later, as they crossed the mouth of a deep bay to the north, Danny scanned the lake with his father's binoculars. "Hey, you guys, wait a minute. I think I see something moving in the water way over there." He pointed due north.

Hank and Mike stopped paddling, letting the canoe drift.

Both squinted in the direction their guide was pointing.

Danny steadied the binoculars and adjusted the focus. "It's a moose! Swimming to that island!" He pointed excitedly to an island maybe a quarter of a mile away. "It's a moose! Let's go!"

Hank turned the canoe north. "Why would a moose be swimming out in the open in the middle of the day?" he wondered out loud. "Let's not come up on it too fast now. We don't want to shock it."

"Do you see it?" Danny asked.

"Ya, I see it now."

"Me too," said Mike. "Looks like a young bull."

"Shhh," Hank cautioned. The canoe slid silently through the water, and slowly, from behind, they gained on the swimming moose, its huge head and horns all that were visible above the water. "Let me get my camera out." Hank unzipped his rucksack.

Then, with the silent moose watchers gliding about fifty yards out from the island, the scraggly-looking animal found footing near the shoreline and climbed unsteadily up onto the rocks. From twenty-five yards out, Danny could see that its long, gangly legs were trembling as it stood on the rocks. "What's wrong," he whispered. "Did we scare him?"

"Look there, at his left rear leg." Hank snapped a picture. "See the blood." An open wound ran down the back of the moose's left rear leg, as if its hide had been ripped away from the bone.

"Wolves?"

"Who knows?"

As Danny leaned over a bit, the binoculars hanging from his neck banged with a pop against the gunwale. The young bull swung its rack toward them with a start, mouth foaming, its eyes glazed with fear. And with a broken jump, it hobbled farther up the rocks and disappeared into the trees on the island.

"Wow! Did you see that?" Danny had never before seen a moose up close in the wild.

"Too bad he won't last the winter, not with that leg." Hank put his camera back into his rucksack. "Let's take a break."

Hank and Mike handed Danny the sierra cups they had hooked to the belts of their trail shorts. Along with his first moose sighting, Danny would eat his first floating trail lunch. He pulled out his Swiss army knife and divvied up the salami, cheese, crackers, chocolate and gorp, with twists of red licorice as an extra treat. They passed the peanut butter by setting the container on the blades of their paddles and moving it between them.

"Foresters leave no trace." They all raised their cups again, then munched their snacks, floating aimlessly in the middle of the bay, talking about the moose.

"I'm going to rename this bay Wounded Moose Bay," Danny announced. "If Dad can name an island, I can name a bay."

"Good man," Hank laughed, and growled a friendly bear growl. His beard had grown thicker and heavier each day, and he was looking more and more like a kind of bear-man.

Mike peeled off his T-shirt, but Danny and his father kept on their life jackets.

When they finished eating, Danny passed around the bug juice. Then he unzipped the map case and stuck three pieces of licorice inside of it to save for later. He set the map and compass on the food pack behind him as he turned to pass the bottle of bug juice back to his father in the stern; and just at that instant, a little gust of wind caught the open map case just right and flipped it into the lake with a blip sound. The case quickly filled with water and started sinking.

"Grab it, Danny!" Hank shouted as the map sunk deeper into the blue-green water and out of Danny's reach. But Danny was afraid of tipping the canoe. So it was Mike, springing like a river otter from his place in the bow, who dove head first into the lake, not even rocking the canoe, chasing after the map.

Danny watched his brother swim underwater, deep into the lake. And after what seemed like too long a time, he finally surfaced behind the stern where Danny couldn't see him.

"I couldn't get it," Mike gasped. He worked his way along the gunwale to the bow. "Hold steady now." Then he pulled himself up into the bow seat, water dripping. He wiped himself off with his T-shirt. "Brrrr, that felt good. We should all go swimming." A twist of red licorice hung from his mouth.

But Danny was left with a kind of sick feeling in his gut, just like he felt when he forgot the cook kit. *Man, I messed up again,* he thought to himself. Not only had he lost their map, but his father's favorite compass, too.

"Okay, trail guide Dan, where to now?" It was his father's teaching voice again, with a touch of sarcasm. "You were in charge of our route. You directed us to this place, chasing after a moose. You lost our map. You lost our compass. Now what do you plan to do?" They sat dead in the water.

Danny looked out over the lake feeling confused and flustered, not quite sure anymore what was an island or a point of land, a bay or an open channel of water.

"Come on, Danny," Mike talked quietly over his shoulder. "You're a smart kid. Use your brain power. Try to remember what the map looked like."

Danny wondered what tests his father had put Mike

through on these trips. Then he decided to take his big brother's advice. So he pulled out his ten-in-one compass device hanging from the lanyard around his neck. He opened up the compass part and took a reading. He knew the wind had been blowing steadily all day from the southeast. He remembered that they had turned due north into the long narrow bay, so they needed to turn south to get back to the main part of the lake. And once they reached the central channel of the lake, he knew they would have to turn and head again to the northwest. He looked up from his compass. "Turn around and follow the right shoreline." He had made his decision.

Hank swept his paddle in huge C-strokes, and aimed the big blue canoe back to the south, into the cross wind. "This may be our last day of sunshine for a while. If this warm humid air meets up with any kind of cold air coming out of the northwest, we're in for some rain."

Danny was glad his father had changed the subject to the weather. He kept silent for nearly the whole hour it took them to paddle back to the part of the lake where they turned once again to the northwest. Because of the moose chase, what had started out as an afternoon of travel would now take them well into the evening. But to Danny, seeing that big moose was worth it, even if he had lost the map.

Back on track with the wind at their back Danny spotted a group of four canoes and paddlers headed their way. "Maybe they have an extra map," he said out loud, not wanting to turn and face his father.

"Don't you dare say one word to those tourists. The last thing I'd ever do is admit we lost our map. That's worse than losing our matches." Hank talked through his teeth.

So there was his answer. The canoeists passed with only a slight nod of the head exchanged between them, honoring each others' desire for solitude.

A little while later Mike called out, "Pull in over here. I wanna' duff for a while and see if I can catch a fish." He pointed to a gravel beach just past a set of low cliffs up ahead. Hank brought them closer to shore, aiming for the beach. But as they passed in front of the lichen-covered flat-rock faces of the cliffs, Danny saw something.

"Hey, what's that?" he pointed.

"Pictographs!" Hank called out from the stern. "Back paddle." The paddlers slowed the canoe to a stop, then sculled sideways toward the cliffs. There, about six feet above the water line, three faint rust-colored images clung to the flat-rock surface, facing south.

"What is it? It looks like a man." Danny pointed to a stick-figure image—head, arms and legs.

"I think it's a Maymaygwayshi."

"Next to a bear?"

"Yes, that looks like a bear."

Each of the ancient rock paintings was only about six or eight inches tall.

"What's that above the bear? A spear?"

"Maybe a lightning bolt." Hank reached for his camera. "Dang, I'm out of film."

"Let's see if there're any more." Danny searched the cliffs with his eyes as the threesome moved forward toward the beach. "Who painted these pictographs, anyway?"

"No one really knows. Maybe hunters, to honor the spirits of the animals who gave their lives to feed them, or warriors, to tell the stories of their victories, or some kind of spiritual leader, like a tribal shaman or medicine man, to mark a sacred place or event."

"I bet it was some prehistoric artist, a crazy guy like Dad." Mike offered his opinion.

"You're right, Mike, I am one of them," Hank said quietly, "and I'd be honored to keep the company of those ancient artists." He dipped his paddle slowly.

At the narrow stretch of gravel, they stepped out into the water, letting the canoe float freely beside them. And as they stood there for a moment, stretching their stiff legs, Danny happened to look back toward the stern seat.

"Hey, what's that?"

Hank smiled. Mike laughed out loud. In the bottom of the canoe, in front of the stern seat, sat the map, map case and compass Danny thought he had lost over the side up Wounded Moose Bay. Mike actually had recovered it, and sneaked it to Hank without Danny seeing. Hank had been using it to guide all along.

"You jerks!" Danny yelled, half laughing at the trick they had played on him. Secretly, though, he was relieved to learn that the map had been saved.

Hank handed him the wet paper. "The day isn't over. You can guide from the bow. Now let's go back and get a picture of that Maymaygwayshi." He had put a new roll of film in his camera.

Mike climbed into the duffer's compartment with his rod and reel. He left the landing net in the bow. Danny found his paddle. Back beside the cliffs they searched for the pictographs.

"Where were they?" Danny scanned back and forth.

"They were right there. I remember that chink in the rock." Hank pointed.

"But they're gone. What happened?"

"I told you. A Maymaygwayshi can disappear into the crevasses between rocks. And, it looks like he took the bear and the lightning bolt with him."

"You know, I'm getting a little tired of tricksters on this

trip." Danny stabbed his paddle into the water and pulled back hard. He would guide them to the northwest, into a maze of islands as the sun moved lower in the sky, still with the wind at their back.

Out in deeper water Mike dropped his huge silver spinner over the side and let it troll behind the canoe. For a long time he played with his line, casting again and again, each time letting the crank bait sink deep into the lake before reeling it in. Then, just as they approached the first of the islands, he hooked a fish. Hank and Danny stopped paddling. Danny popped open the landing net.

Mike expertly played the fish, taking his time, letting it run out line, then slowly reeling it back in, to and fro, wearing it down. Eventually Danny caught a glimpse of it near the surface—a magnificent lake trout, up from the depths, magical-looking, like no fish he had ever seen before. Mike netted it himself.

"Dinner," he announced, as he attached the stringer to its jaw. Then he held his catch up with both hands for Danny to examine. But Danny didn't see food so much as beauty. In the late afternoon sunlight the glistening scales of the speckled gray fish gave off a kind of multicolored iridescence that reminded him of his pine knot fire.

Mike dropped the trout back into the water, holding onto the stringer. Danny turned forward in the bow and pointed to a channel between two islands where the shadows had already fallen. "There," he said confidently. "There's where we want to go." He had gotten the scale of the map into his head. He had become a trail guide like his father and his brother.

chapter seven

BEAR SCARE

With Kawnipi behind them, the only campsite they could find for the night sat on low ground in a stand of cedar trees not far from a shallow gurgling rapids. Already working in the shadows of dusk, they set their gear on shore, more like a riverbank in the narrows between the mainland and an island. Deep moss grew everywhere. Hank and Mike two-manned the canoe across the campsite, turning it over and gently setting it down back and away from the fire pit. The only tent site was barely big enough, but would have to do.

As his father surveyed the campsite, Danny noticed him frowning, wearing his serious dad face. "Look here," he called out to his sons, shaking his head.

Mike and Danny hustled over to where he was standing. Hank pointed out a series of overturned rocks, pulled out of the ground by a bear digging for grubs. "He's been through here very recently, since the rain." Then he pointed to a big cedar tree. "See there." The bark up one side of the tree had been shredded, clawed by the bear to mark its territory. "It's too late to look for another campsite in these waters. We better hang the food pack. Feel free to make as much noise as you want."

"Look over here!" Danny called out excitedly. In the ash-mud of the fire pit, he had found a huge paw print, even showing the claws. "Wow! Take a picture of that."

Hank did take a picture, then started a fire, a big fire. Mike gutted his prized trout, but threw the entrails into the flames instead of leaving them for scavengers. He smeared the fish with butter and wrapped it in double foil to bake in the hot coals. Hank cooked up pots of rice and freeze-dried peas, with butterscotch pudding for dessert. No bread this night. The idea was to finish dinner as quickly as possible, burn every scrap of leftovers, get the dishes cleaned and then string the food pack for the night. Danny worked on the tent.

"You guys wait here. We need more firewood. Danny, give me your whistle." While the fish baked, Hank disappeared into the dark forest in search of more firewood, blowing Danny's bear whistle every few steps.

Danny was surprised by the intensity of his father's reaction to the signs of a bear. "What's with Dad?" he asked Mike.

"Oh, he gets kinda freaked out by campsite bears. Don't let him rattle you. He'll settle down."

Danny could feel his own stomach tighten a bit, thinking about his father out in the woods, nearly dark now. Then, after what seemed like a long time, he heard the crack of a branch and jumped up, but heard the whistle again and knew it was his father.

Hank Forester trudged out of the woods hauling two skinny downed and dead jack pine trees, one under each arm, holding them by their small root wads. Sweat poured off his face. His arms and legs were covered with scratches. He hadn't yet changed out of his trail shorts and T-shirt. Danny and Mike each grabbed one of the trees and dragged them over by the fire.

"This should do it for a bear-fire tonight," Hank announced grimly, as he wiped his brow. He didn't say anything about the scratches or how tired he must have felt. "Let's eat."

Mike broke open his baked trout, done to perfection. The three of them stood around the fire and ate ravenously, downing two bottles of lemonade as well.

"The blueberry crop failed this year, and the raspberries. These bears are hungry and trying to fatten up for winter." Hank talked between bites of fish. "They're looking for anything to eat." He glanced over his shoulder toward the trees behind them, almost night now. "Let's hope this one was just passing through and is miles from here tonight."

They hurriedly rinsed off the dishes in cold water. Then Hank closed up the food pack along with their toothpaste and soap, which a bear could smell, too. He stuck a sturdy branch, about four feet long, across the top of the pack before he strapped the top flap down. The stick stuck out about a foot on either side of the pack. Meanwhile, Mike had taken the rope and climbed a big cedar tree overhanging the shallow rapids. At the campsite crowded with trees, it was the only possible place to hang the food pack.

"Come on, Danny, I need your help."

Danny followed his father out into the moving water, ankle deep and slippery.

"You got good footing."

"Yeah."

"Good. Now, I just want you to hold the pack up while I tie on the rope."

Danny took the pack in his arms, surprised to find how much less it now weighed—or had he become that much stronger? Mike dropped the rope down from the tree. Hank tied the rope to the ends of the thick stick. "Okay, pull it up."

Mike slowly hoisted up the food pack. Hank stood below it, swatting his hands in the air like bear paws until the pack was out of reach.

"That's good enough."

Mike knotted the rope, then climbed back down the tree. The pack swung freely above the water. They all met back at the fire. Night had fallen.

It had worked out to be a longer, harder day than they had planned, but Danny wasn't ready to turn in. The signs of a bear in the area had gotten his adrenaline pumped up. He was still wearing his trail shorts and T-shirt, and against the heat of the fire he noticed he had sunburned the fronts of his legs and arms, so he turned his back to the flames. He glanced at his tent pitching job, door open to the fire. Then he looked over at the old White Otter, his eyes adjusting to the dark. And there, peering at him out of the night, with one great paw resting on his father's canoe, stood a huge black bear.

Danny gulped as his heart slammed up into this throat. He felt for his whistle. Gone. "Dad, Mike," he stammered, pointing to the bear.

"Get away from my canoe!" Hank picked up a rock.

"Don't throw it, Dad, you might hit the canoe." Mike tried to calm his father down.

The bear didn't move. Hank grabbed the ax and started whacking off branches of jack pine and piling them onto the fire, flames flaring up high, sparks shooting into the night sky. This got the bear's attention. It backed away from the canoe and moved into the shadows. But Danny could still see its fiery eyes.

"Geez, he's a big male. I bet he weighs five hundred pounds. See how healthy his fur looks." Hank flashed his camera off in rapid succession, which only seemed to make the bear more curious.

Then Hank and Mike began clapping their hands and stomping their feet at the bear. Danny stood between them and banged on a pot with a spoon, all three yelling and waving their arms as they moved behind the fire. This only seemed to anger the hairy brute, because all at once it lowered its ears back and slapped the ground hard with its right front paw. The ground shook. Danny shook.

"He's bluffing." Hank stomped his foot hard again.

"I dunno', Dad," Mike cautioned. "Let's make sure he has room to escape."

But the big black bear showed no sign of leaving.

"Quiet!" Hank yelled.

In the instant silence Danny could hear the bear making a kind of blowing sound, and clacking its teeth at them. The three campers pressed together. Danny picked up a rock in each hand. Mike threw a stubby log into the trees, but instead of running away, the bear lunged, bursting a short distance toward the intruders into its territory, smacking the ground hard again with its right paw. At this, Hank broke from beside Danny, screaming as loud as he could, ax raised high in the air, leaping over the fire and charging forward—a half-crazed bear-man chasing an angry bear.

"Noooo!" Mike screamed as he flew through the air and tackled his father halfway between the fire and the bear. They both crashed onto the rocks, Mike holding his father down. The bear reared up on its hind legs, growled loudly and swiped at the air with its paws.

"Don't move!" Danny shouted to his father and brother. Across the raging fire Danny stood alone against the bear. Every muscle in his body was trembling. He had no idea what to do. But then, a very mysterious thing happened. As he and the bear stared at each other, Danny felt a strange sense of familiarity. *I know this bear,* was his thought. *He's one of the bears from my dreams, my bearmares.* And in Danny's mind the bear seemed to be saying: *I know you, kid. Why are you so afraid? You have nothing to fear from me.*

Danny dropped the rocks he was holding. The big bear dropped down onto all fours, turned and disappeared into the night. They could hear it crashing through the dense pine forest until there was silence—except for the sound of the crackling fire—and the beating of their hearts.

Hank stood up. "I'm sorry guys. That was stupid of me. I went kinda berserk there."

"No kidding. Were you trying to get us all killed or just commit suicide?" Mike was angry at his father.

"What are we going to do?" Danny asked, his heart still racing, not quite believing he had nothing to fear from the bear.

"Nothing to do but keep a bear-fire." Hank picked up the ax.

Mike assessed their wood pile. "Dad, this isn't going to last the night."

"I know," Hank responded, "but these will." He kicked one of a half dozen log benches some previous campers had constructed around the fire pit. "In case of bear trouble, you can burn anything that burns." He picked up the bow saw and started sawing a foot and a half section off the end of one of the thick logs.

So into the night they sawed and chopped, sawed and chopped, taking turns until they had worked off their fear and their anger. Only occasionally did they stop to look and listen for any bear lurking on the fringes of their fire-lighted world. No signs of trouble.

Danny sat exhausted on top of a pile of split firewood.

"Why don't you guys turn in?" Hank passed the water bottle around. "I think we're okay. I think that big fella' just wanted to get a look at us. He's probably miles away by now, raiding some other campsite."

Danny wasn't sure he wanted to go into the tent, but he was too tired to argue with his father.

"Let's go, kid." Mike handed him a wet towel to wipe off the dirt and sweat. "Dad can handle this."

The two brothers headed into the tent, leaving their trail boots outside. The night had turned cool. Once inside his sleeping bag, Danny sunk deep into the soft moss beneath the tent—too tired to worry about a bear, or to think about what had happened. He fell asleep in an instant.

Sometime around three in the morning Danny woke up. He could hear his father breaking jack pine branches with his feet. He got up, pulled on his campsite shoes and walked over to the fire.

"Hey, camper. What are you doing up?" Hank was still wearing his boots and trail shorts, but he had pulled on Mike's Quetico sweatshirt.

"I just woke up and couldn't get back to sleep."

"Well sit down." Hank poured Danny a cup of coffee, then they sat together on what was left of one of the log benches. The big teepee fire sent sparks up between the tree branches above them.

"I think he's gone for the night," Hank tried to reassure Danny. "I'm just kinda' having fun with the fire."

"Good. You had me frightened there for a while." Danny took only a sip of the bitter coffee.

Hank didn't say anything for a few minutes, then he spoke up. "Danny, let me tell you a story." They both poked at the fire with long sticks.

"When I was about your age my father took me on a one-week canoe trip through the White Otter chain of lakes. On those trips he used to love to read me Robert Service poems at night around the fire, or in the tent if the mosquitoes were too bad. Robert Service was his favorite Canadian poet.

"One night he read me a poem titled *The Men That Don't Fit In*. I'll never forget it. But what my father didn't know, was that I had sneaked a chocolate bar from the trail lunch into the tent with me. I thought I might get hungry during the night. He had even strung up our food pack because he knew there was a bear on the lake we were camped on. But I didn't believe that a bear could smell just one chocolate bar.

"Later, we both fell asleep. I remember I was dreaming about a great silver fish in the water, when all of a sudden I heard my father yell out. And when I opened up my eyes, I saw against the moonlight that a big black bear had ripped open the side of our tent and stuck his head in. I couldn't speak or move or do anything. I was paralyzed with fear. But my father started punching that bear in its nose as hard as he could. He was a man with big strong hands, fists like sledge-hammers, and he yelled and swore and hammered on that old bear's nose until it backed its head out of the tent and ran off into the woods.

"Next my father found his flashlight and turned it on me, to see if I was okay. And he saw my chocolate bar. He grabbed it and threw it after the bear. I'd never seen him so mad at me, though now I know that he was probably just very frightened, for me and for himself. But that night, it was his fierceness that saved us.

"For a long time after that I had frightening dreams of being chased by bears. I didn't want to tell anyone about these nightmares because I was ashamed about how I hadn't helped my father chase off the bear, and I didn't want anyone to know that I was still afraid of bears. I thought I was a coward.

"But my mother knew something was wrong, so I told her about the dreams. She was always easier to talk to than my father. He was smart with his hands, but she was wise with her heart. She knew about what had happened with the bear and my father. We had told her. But she had a different idea about what the dreams might mean. She said that because I was adopted the bears chasing me in my dreams might be my ancestors trying to make contact with me. She said that I was at least a fourth-blood Anishinabe. Maybe my Native American ancestors were a part of a bear clan? Maybe they were searching for their lost son? She said it was all right with her if some day I wanted to find my biological parents, but I never have wanted to. I loved the mother and father who raised me, and I miss them.

"Anyway, the dreams stopped as suddenly as they had started, and I sort of forgot about them. But for some reason, in the last two years or so, the bears chasing me in my dreams have returned. I haven't figured out why."

Hank stirred the fire to let more air through.

"Danny, I worry that this fear of bears that has lived inside of me for so long somehow got inside of you. This happens sometimes. It's kind of a mystery—how a fear inside of a father can get inside of his son without the father ever telling the son about this fear. You see, I think that your fear of bears is really my fear of bears. So I'm sorry I didn't tell you this story before."

Danny wasn't sure he understood what his father was talking about. He kept silent, looking down at the ground.

"Forget it, camper." Hank threw another log on the fire. "Would you like to hear a poem? How about just one?" He pulled a thin volume of Robert Service verse out of his rucksack.

"The Cremation of Sam McGee," Danny requested his favorite.

And so, Hank began:

> *"There are strange things done in the midnight sun*
> *By the men who moil for gold;*
> *The Arctic trails have their secret tales*
> *That would make your blood run cold;*
> *The Northern Lights have seen queer sights,*
> *But the queerest they ever did see*
> *Was the night on the marge of Lake Lebarge*
> *I cremated Sam McGee."*

He read the whole thing through, then he tossed yet another log on the fire. Turning to Danny he talked some more about bears. "You know, Danny, in all my years of camping up here, I've only heard about one bear attack in the Boundary Waters—a half-crazed starving old sow who bit a camper on the leg. No one's ever been killed that I know of. Sure, an occasional campsite bear gets into a bad habit of raiding food packs, but actual bear attacks on humans are extremely rare. I don't really know what I've been so afraid of; and I'm sorry I frightened you."

"I'm okay, Dad." Danny kicked a burning ember back into the fire, thinking about what had happened earlier that night. "Thanks for telling me the story about camping with your father. I don't think you were chicken. You were just a kid, like me. You did the best you could."

"Ya, I guess you're right." Hank closed his Robert Service book. "Well, look, it's very late, almost four o'clock. You better get back to sleep." He gave Danny a shoulder hug and tousled his sandy-brown hair. They both growled a friendly father-son growl. Above them, amongst the star-speckled sky, the northern constellations Ursa Major and Ursa Minor — the Great Bear and the Little Bear, also known as the Big Dipper and the Little Dipper—sparkled brightly through the treetops.

Feeling tired again, Danny stood up and started back to the tent. Then he stopped and turned to his father. "Dad, when we get home, will you paint a picture of a black bear for me?"

Hank looked at him for a moment, thinking. "Sure I will, Danny. It's a promise I will keep." He reached into his rucksack and took out a small sketchbook and a box of pencils. "Get some sleep now." He looked up at his son. Danny crawled back into the tent, like a yearling cub crawling into its den.

chapter eight

KAHSHAHPIWI STORM

In the morning Danny and Mike found their father asleep next to the dead fire. His head rested on a charred rock. His legs sprawled halfway into the cold ashes. All of the firewood had been burned.

While their father slept in the ashes, Mike lowered the food pack into Danny's arms. Over their one-burner stove the two of them cooked a breakfast of oatmeal, with bits of dried fruit and brown sugar, along with a pot of cocoa. Danny filtered water from the lake and mixed up another bottle of freeze-dried orange juice.

It took them several minutes to rouse their father out of the ashes. Eventually he stood up, shakily, and dusted himself off. But he seemed only half-awake, not interested in eating. He drank a cup of orange juice, then went and stood in the shallow rapids, washing off his legs.

Danny and Mike broke camp quickly, without starting a fire. Mike poured water on the pile of ashes in the fire pit to make sure there were no hot coals left behind. At this site they would not bury their wet ashes or leave a neat stack of firewood for the next campers. Danny packed up the cook kit without even washing it. Mike flipped up the big blue canoe and walked it into the water.

With the boat floating empty, Hank half-crawled, half-fell into the stern compartment where the packs usually sat. He curled up between the cedar ribs, laid his head down on his rucksack and closed his eyes. Mike loaded the packs into the bow compartment where the duffer usually sat. Then Danny and Mike walked the canoe upstream through the rapids until the cold flowing water came up past their knees. Danny climbed into the bow with the map and compass. Mike pushed the eighteen-footer forward with a strong shove as he took the stern.

"Paddle hard now!" he called out to Danny as they worked against the current of Kahshahpiwi Creek.

Their goal was to reach a campsite on the south end of Kahshahpiwi Lake—a long day's paddle and a half dozen portages away. The sky had turned a hazy blue. It was hard to know from what direction the wind was blowing, much cooler, though, than the day before.

It was their fifth day on the trail. Danny recalled his father talking about how, after about four days on a canoe trip, he would shed all thoughts of city life. It would start to feel like he had lived in the wilderness forever. Danny now knew what his father was talking about. On this fifth day he felt no homesickness at all, except he missed cold milk from the refrigerator. Instead, he felt alert and strong in the bow, and had come to prefer paddling over duffing. He checked the map.

At the first portage, Mike poked Hank awake. The big man climbed out of the canoe, grabbed only his rucksack and stumbled along the trail like he was sleep-walking. Mike lifted the food pack for Danny to carry. He set the other packs on shore. Next, he flipped the canoe up onto his shoulders and led his brother up the portage path. Danny hadn't realized how well Mike could also flip and carry the canoe.

At the other end of the portage Mike walked into the water and flipped down. He took the food pack from Danny and set it again in the bow compartment. Hank followed and stood knee deep, holding the canoe. "I got it," was all he said. Then Danny and Mike hustled back over the portage to retrieve the rest of the gear.

And so they traveled, the sons carrying the father, a slumbering human cargo, upstream along the Kahshahpiwi chain of lakes—Cairn, Sark, Keefer, connected by Kahshahpiwi Creek, all running south-by-southwest to north-by-northeast in a straight line. Unlike the open expanses of water on Saganaga and Kawnipi, this narrow stretch of lakes sat low between high ridges covered with thick stands of towering pines that only added to the upward thrust of the landscape. On the map, it looked to Danny like the giant who had fallen dead face-first into Saganagons, had at one time sunk a huge ax blade into the rock of the Canadian Shield, forming Kahshahpiwi, like a deep ax-wound in the earth, half-filled with glacial waters.

By midday the hazy sky had turned gray with clouds. The travelers stopped on the south end of their fifth portage, between Cairn and Keefer Lakes. Time for trail lunch. And here, Hank seemed to come alive again.

"Thanks for carrying me, guys. I just couldn't seem to wake up. I think that whole bear thing sorta' wiped me out." He chewed on a piece of salami.

"Couldn't it be that you haven't slept for the past five nights?" Mike still seemed angry at his father.

Hank ignored the comment. "Looks like rain."

Danny was glad to have his father back.

As they sat there eating, a single canoe approached them from the south. Two women paddled up, a younger woman paddling stern and an older woman paddling bow, perhaps mother and daughter. They were traveling light, one pack and a lightweight canoe. They greeted the threesome. Then the young woman took the canoe, followed by the older woman with the pack on her back. As they walked past, the older woman looked directly at Danny. "Good luck on Yum Yum Portage," she smiled, and kept hiking up the trail.

Danny noticed that her trail pants were stained with mud from the knees down. *How did she know we planned to cross Yum Yum Portage?* he thought to himself. Her words sounded more like a warning than a good luck wish.

After lunch Danny duffed, Mike returned to the bow and Hank took his place back in the stern. They crossed Keefer Lake and took the last portage into Kahshahpiwi. Hank carried canoe. Mike double-packed. Danny remembered the cook kit.

"Ahh, Kahshahpiwi." Hank stood looking out at what he could see of the lake from the end of the portage. "My favorite of all Quetico lakes. I don't know why, but I love Kahshahpiwi best."

From a small bay at the north end of the lake a tight narrows led them south along a high ridge jutting up steeply, two hundred feet from the water, to the main body of the lake. Here, Danny thought, the giant's ax blows must have sunk deepest into the rock. Surrounded by walls of towering pines, and covered by a low ceiling of clouds, Kahshahpiwi became yet another world unto itself—deeply mysterious, a lake that held secrets. Knowing his moody father, Danny understood immediately why he would love moody Kahshahpiwi.

An hour and a half later they found the campsite they had wanted, set high off the lake in a stand of red pine on a peninsula not far from Yum Yum Portage. The wind picked up out of the west just as they landed. Hank looked up at the sky. "Let's gather as much firewood as we can. Come on."

All three carried the canoe up into the campsite, setting it down on a bed of pine needles behind two huge tree trunks. They turned its belly into the wind to prevent it from being blown away in the storm. Hank helped with the tent, rocking-out one corner and adding extra ropes to the rain fly. They positioned the tent with its back wall to the wind. Hank made doubly sure the tent wasn't pitched near any standing dead trees that could topple onto them in the night.

Then the three of them hunted for firewood together, carrying armloads out from deep in the forest behind the campsite. The rain held off. Because of the high ridges it was impossible to see what was coming at them from the west, but the low rumble of distant thunder forewarned them. They worked steadily.

Hank boiled water in the biggest cook kit pot to clean the breakfast dishes. He used his reflector oven as a windbreak for the camp stove, and concocted another one of his one-pot stews—beef stroganoff and noodles, with a no-bake chocolate dessert he called "Quetico Delight." Danny helped Mike stow the paddles and life jackets under the canoe along with their wet trail boots. They had all changed into long pants, dry socks and their campsite shoes. The rain jackets were ready by the tent.

"Let's try to get in the tent while we're all still dry," Hank advised. "That way we'll at least be halfway comfortable. Did you bring your playing cards, Danny?"

"Yes, sir." To Danny it seemed like his father had regained his senses and was back in charge of things.

They ate hurriedly as the sky darkened. Along with the rumbling of thunder, flashes of lightning now skittered across the ridge line to the west. The wind had steadily grown stronger. The great red pines spoke to the clouds in loud whispers, sweeping back and forth, back and forth. An occasional branch fell from the sky. The tent flapped. They cleaned up their dishes as quickly as they could and packed up for the night.

Mike found room under the canoe for the equipment pack. Hank stuffed the cook kit inside the food pack and strapped it down tightly. He kept out the first aid kit to treat a burn on his thumb. Then he covered the pack with a tarp, and tied it securely to a tree trunk, facing it away from the lake. Danny organized what was left of the firewood and covered it with the ash-tarp, held in place by big stones.

It was nearly seven o'clock, and getting darker. But they stood around the fire talking about Mike's fish, Danny's bear and Yum Yum Portage, until the first big drops of rain began to sweep across the lake toward them. Then they dashed headlong into the tent, each collapsing onto his own sleeping bag.

"One game of Uno," Hank offered.

Danny pulled out a fresh deck of cards from the bottom of his sleeping bag. He handed it to Mike to shuffle and deal. Meanwhile, he unloaded his pocket survival gear and put it all in the stuff sack for his sleeping bag, as he had done every night. Next, he changed into his sweat suit.

Mike dealt. The three players sat cross-legged and laughed and laughed at each hand, accusing each other of cheating. They played until it was too dark to see the cards and the scent of the rain had overtaken the smell of wood smoke. Danny won.

Hank used his flashlight to find burn cream and a burn bandage. Then he used the first aid kit as a pillow for his head. He laid back with a groan and fell instantly to sleep. Mike was fast asleep, too. He had paddled nearly sixteen miles that day, and carried the canoe over five portages. Danny laid down between his father and brother, thinking. Five days—he had made it halfway—caught the biggest fish, spotted a moose and stood up to a bear. Tomorrow he would face Yum Yum Portage, the Quetico's toughest climb. But he felt stronger now, more confident somehow. Besides, the food pack was much lighter. Soon enough, he fell asleep to the sound of the falling rain.

CRACK-BOOM! CRACK-BOOM! Danny was jolted awake like he'd been knocked into the air and dropped down again. CRACK-CRACK-KA-BOOM! Thunder and lightning danced right on top of the tent—a mean dance. CRACK-BOOM! Black night. CRACK-BOOM! White light.

"Are you guys awake?"

Hank and Mike were sleeping through the storm. Danny listened for their breathing to make sure they hadn't been killed by a lightning strike. He'd heard about how lightning could follow tree roots and kill people inside their tent. CRACK-BOOM! CRACK-BOOM! He felt for his flashlight. Nothing to do but lie there and take it in—the power of the storm. BOOM-BOOM-BOOM! The wind strained the tent ropes.

Then a long crackle of lightning ended in a deafening explosion—CRAAACK! BOOOM! Sparks flew out of the sky as the upper forty feet of a flaming red pine came crashing down hard upon the tent.

"What the... ? Oh, no!" Both Hank and Mike awoke screaming in pain.

A half ton of smoldering wood had landed on Hank's lower legs, missing Danny's feet by inches, and a spear-like broken branch on that same log had impaled Mike's right ankle, pinning him to the ground.

"I can't move!" Mike screamed, face down.

"Me neither!" cried Hank. "I think my legs are broken. I'm hurt! I'm hurt bad! Danny! Where are you?"

"I... I... I'm okay. I'm here. I'm not hurt." He turned on his flashlight, heart pounding, hands shaking. The tent fabric had come down on top of them. Water seeped in from the folds of nylon.

"Danny, listen. This is bad, a real bad situation." Hank tried to talk calmly, gasping for breath, wincing in pain. CRACK-CRACK! BOOM-BOOM! The storm raged on. "You gotta' get outside and move that tree off of our legs, and you gotta do it now!"

Mike was able to turn on his side and hold part of the wet tent up with his arms. "Where's your knife, little brother?"

"Right here." Danny opened the big blade to his Swiss army knife.

"Well, hurry up! Cut your way outta' here!" Hank grabbed Danny's arm, digging in his finger nails to make his point.

"Settle down, Dad!" Mike loosened Hank's grip on Danny's arm. "He can do this." Then he pulled Danny's face close to his. "Get the paddles so we have something to hold up the tent when you move the tree. You got that?"

"Yes."

"Where's your rain jacket?"

"Right here."

"Put it on."

"Shoes?"

"I don't know."

"Here, take mine."

Danny hurriedly pulled on his brother's big shoes. CRACK-BOOM! CRACK-BOOM! The tent lit up like daylight. He could see the suffering on his father's face, like an animal caught in a steel leg trap, eyes wild with pain.

"Get going!" Hank commanded, almost screaming through clinched teeth. "Now!"

"But what am I supposed to do?" Danny stammered, his whole body trembling.

"Move the tree!"

"But, how?"

"I don't know how! Just do it!" Hank was screaming, now, red-faced.

"Danny," Mike spoke in a calmer, but serious voice, "you gotta' suck a gut here." He sounded just like Coach Jones. He took Danny's knife and cut a slit in the floor of the tent along the back wall, then handed the knife back to his brother. "You can do this."

Danny nodded his head, but inside himself he felt scared,

not confident. He grabbed Mike's flashlight. Then, as quickly as he could, he crawled outside into the driving wind and rain. CRACK-BOOM! White lightning flashed right at treetop level, illuminating the scene—tree branches everywhere. He could smell burning wood, ignited by the lightning bolt.

CRACK-BOOM! This time closer, brighter, hotter. *I'm dead.* Danny thought to himself. *I'm a dead kid.* He crawled over the branches, imagining his death by lightning strike. The searchers would find his body out in the open, half-eaten by a bear, his brother and father stone-cold dead in the tent.

Slipping, falling, half-crawling, he made his way to the old White Otter, luckily undamaged as far as he could tell. He ran his hands across the wet belly of the canoe. From beneath it he pulled out the three paddles, cradling them in his arms as he ran back to the tent, praying not to get struck by lightning.

"I got 'em. Here they come." Danny slid his paddle and Mike's paddle in through the slit in the tent floor.

"Get that tree off of us!" Hank called out. "We're dying in here."

Danny gripped his father's long, T-handled paddle. On the square blade, Hank had painted a pictograph of an eagle—a thunderbird. Danny found a spot to wedge the paddle beneath the splintered red pine. Rain soaked his hair and face. The wet ground squished beneath his feet. Putting his shoulder under the shaft of the paddle, he pushed hard with his legs to lever the log off the tent, but the tree wouldn't budge. BOOM! BOOM! BOOM! CRACK! CRACK! CRACK! In the flashes of lightning, he could see that a big branch was preventing the log from rolling over.

"Hurry up!" His father cried out.

As fast as he could, his sweat pants soaked below his jacket, Danny made his way back to the canoe and pulled the bow saw out from the equipment pack. CRACK! FLASH! BEAR! There by the food pack. Black as the night. Huge. *I'm dead. I'm a dead kid.* CRACK! FLASH! NO BEAR! No time to waste. No time to feel fear. Suck a gut. Just do it.

He tore off the saw sheath as he ran back to the downed tree, where he sawed without stopping until the big branch broke loose. Again he jammed his father's paddle underneath the smoldering tree trunk and put his shoulder into it. Snap! The paddle blade broke.

CRACK-BOOM! White light. CRACK-BOOM! BLACK BEAR! There—just ten feet away—pushing its front paws against the splintered tree. Powerful shoulders. No time for fear. Suck a gut. Just do it. BOOM! BOOM! BOOM! Danny jammed the laminated shaft even farther under the log, this time pushing with all his might and letting out a deep bear growl as the massive half tree rolled off and away from the tent. CRACK! FLASH! NO BEAR! What had just happened? Had he imagined the bear? Twice?

"Ohhh! Ohhh!" No time to think about it. Danny could hear both men moaning in pain from inside the tent. Quickly he crawled back inside the sagging structure.

"Dad, don't try to move. Let me check Mike's ankle. We've got to stop any bleeding first." Danny propped up both canoe paddles like tent poles. This worked to hold the tent up. Then he examined Mike's ankle.

"Here." Hank pushed the first aid kit over to Danny.

Mike was sitting up holding his ankle. Four gauze pads from Danny's mini first aid kit were already soaked with blood. Down feathers flew everywhere. The sharp branch had torn through Mike's sleeping bag as well as the tent. But worse, it had completely punctured Mike's right ankle, between his ankle bones and his Achilles' tendon. Blood oozed from both sides of the wound. Rain dripped inside the tent.

"Lie back down, Mike. I have to elevate your leg to help stop the bleeding." Danny bunched up his own sleeping bag under Mike's lower legs. Then he opened up the first aid kit. He knew just where to find the pressure bandages. Quickly he pressed the thick compresses on the opposite sides of Mike's ankle, taping them down securely. "Don't move," he told Mike. "Shine your light over at Dad." Then he turned toward his father.

Hank looked at Danny in the dim light. Beads of sweat had formed across his forehead. "I know they're broken. It hurts too much to move them. Check for bleeding. Check for pulses in my ankles."

"I know," said Danny. With broken legs, his mother had taught him to check for pulses in the ankles. No pulse, or a weak pulse, might indicate internal bleeding—a very bad sign. Someone could bleed to death from a broken leg before help reached them.

As carefully as he could, Danny pulled away his father's sleeping bag.

"Ow! Ow! Ow!"

"I'm sorry." Danny shined his flashlight on Hank's lower legs. "The skin's not broken, but they definitely look messed up."

"They feel messed up."

"The right break looks higher up, between your knee and your ankle. The left break is more down by the ankle."

"I know. That's where I can feel the pain." Hank winced again. "Ouch."

"Sorry." Danny concentrated. "The pulses in both feet are strong. Here, take these." He handed his father two pills from a prescription bottle in the first aid kit. "Mom said these are for serious pain, like broken bones."

"Thanks." Hank took the pills without water.

Danny gave two of the same pills to Mike. Then he turned back to his father. "Dad, I'm going to splint both of your legs now, and treat you for shock. You have to elevate your legs and keep warm."

Danny took two inflatable splints out of the first aid kit— one full leg splint and one ankle splint. Painstakingly, he applied the splints to this father's legs, just as his mother had taught him to do. He blew through the air valves until the splints inflated enough to stabilize the breaks along with the knee and ankle joints. Then he took the empty personal pack, rolled it up and slid it under his father's legs to elevate them. Finally, he covered his father with his sleeping bag.

"How's the pain?"

"A little better, maybe. I don't know. Thanks, doc."

The worst of the storm had passed. Danny wasn't even sure what time it was, or how soon dawn would come. He turned off Mike's flashlight to save on batteries, and knelt between his father and brother in the dark tent. "What are we going to do now, campers?" He didn't dare say anything about a cell phone, or a GPS device, or the bear he thought he saw outside in the storm.

"We're going to fall back on our training," was Mike's answer. "Remember what Mom taught us. S.T.O.P. Stay-Think-Organize-Plan."

"I just wish Mom was here."

"Danny," Hank spoke up, "your mother is here. She's been with us in spirit the whole time."

"But I want her here with us now, for real, not just in spirit. She's a doctor, an emergency room doctor. We need her." Danny could feel a terrible fear again well up inside of his chest.

"Listen, Danny, it's like Mike said, you just gotta' suck a gut here. You're the only one who can get done what needs to get done to get us out of here." Hank winced through his teeth as he talked. "You want your mother here? Okay then, think, Danny, how would Mom handle this?"

Danny could hear his mother's voice. *It all starts with clear thinking,* she would say. *The life of the patient may depend on a doctor who can think clearly in the middle of an emergency.*

"She would tell us to calm down and think clearly." Danny took in a deep breath. In that moment he realized that their very survival rested on his shoulders, like the weight of his father's canoe. Could he bear this burden? Could he save his father? Inside of himself he asked this question, and inside of himself came the answer. *Yes,* he said to himself. And with that, he could feel the first inklings of a newly-found courage pushing aside his fear.

"Like I said," Mike repeated himself in the dark tent. "Stay-Think-Organize-Plan."

"So, what *is* the plan?" Danny asked.

"Well," Hank spoke again, "for all we know we could be the last campers on Kahshahpiwi for the season. Unless we plan to spend the winter here, you and Mike are going to have to go get help—at first light."

But how? Danny thought to himself. *How are we ever going to make it across Yum Yum Portage?*

chapter nine

YUM YUM RUN

They worked out a survival plan. Danny would have to organize everything while Mike rested his ankle to stop the bleeding. Hank could not be moved.

The thunder and lightning had passed, but a cold rain fell steadily. While it was still dark, working by flashlight, Danny pulled on his trail jeans and boots. Then he took the tarp covering the food pack and tied it down over the hole in the tent to stop the leak. Next, he found their two water bottles and filled them with lake water, handing one each to his father and brother. They needed to drink water to help prevent shock.

In the first light of dawn he straightened out, as best he could, the bent aluminum tent poles. But the front of the tent still sagged, so he strung the big rope between two red pine trees. Using a shorter piece of rope, he attached the top front corner of the tent to the big rope. This worked to free up the paddles holding up the tent from the inside. He took the paddles, along with two life jackets, and set them down by the lake.

The ash-tarp had kept some of the wood dry, so Danny built a fire in the rain. Hunkered over a meager pile of damp sticks and shredded birch bark, he carefully removed his packet of waxed matches from his pocket. Peeling the wax away from the red match heads, he struck the first match. It blew out before it touched the wood. The second match lit a corner of the birch bark, but the damp sticks would not ignite. Danny leaned with his rain jacket hanging open over the fire pit. He struck the third match, cupping his hands around the small flame. Slowly, ever so slowly, all the birch bark caught fire and produced enough heat to start the sticks burning. He blew gently onto the flames, carefully adding more wood until the fire took on a life of its own. He knew it wouldn't last long, but there was something comforting about having a fire.

Over by the canoe, he dismantled his father's reflector oven. It had been a wedding gift to Hank and Maddy from a fellow trail guide at the youth camp. Hank had kept it in perfect condition all of these years—not one dent. Using the butt of the ax head, Danny hammered on the two biggest rectangles of aluminum, shaping them against a rock to fit against the bottom of the canoe. Hank had instructed him how to fashion a kind of drag-plate, and fasten it with duct tape below the stern. Danny would have to drag the canoe on this plate of aluminum over the portages to prevent sharp rocks from tearing through the canvas.

He dried off the bottom of the stern with a T-shirt from the personal pack. And again using his jacket to block the rain, he taped the aluminum shield in place. Then he wrapped more tape all around the stern, top to bottom, securing the shield, until he had used nearly half the roll of duct tape from the equipment pack. He saved the rest of the tape to make a cast for Mike's right ankle.

Next, he took the shelf from the reflector oven, bent it at a right angle and hammered it into the shape of a brace for Mike's foot. He hustled back to the tent, ankle brace and duct tape in hand.

"Here, Mike, try this on." Mike's foot was already swollen. The pressure bandages showed blood.

"Ouch!" Mike winced. "Careful."

Danny wrapped a whole roll of two-inch medical tape around the ankle, holding it stiffly in place. He covered the taped-up bandages with a big plastic bag from the food pack. Then he cut open Mike's right shoe, slipped the sole over Mike's foot, and fit the metal brace in place. All of this he wrapped in duct tape, forming a make-shift cast.

"We'll have to call you Silver Foot."

"Thanks, brother."

Hank's broken T-handled paddle made a perfect crutch. Danny helped Mike stand up outside the tent. He tied the laces for his brother's left trail boot.

"As much as possible, we have to try to keep this foot dry and elevated." Danny tapped Mike's wounded foot.

"I know." Mike leaned over and stuck his head in the tent. "Dad, we'll be back before dark, or sooner. Don't worry, I'll watch out for Danny."

Hank reached up, clasped Mike's hand in a soul-shake and nodded his head. Mike limped down to the shoreline.

Danny crawled inside the tent. In one hand he carried the big pot from the cook kit, half-filled with water, and the rest of the cook kit in its canvas bag.

In the other hand he held the one-burner stove and a box

of matches. "If you get cold, start this up, but not for too long without some ventilation in here. And drink water." Then he covered his father with his own sleeping bag, the one that had been rolled up under Mike's legs. "How're you doing?"

"Okay. I'm going to be okay." Hank tried to reassure his son. "How about you?"

"I don't know, Dad. It kills me to know what we're going to do to your canoe—drag it on the rocks." Danny's eyes filled with tears.

"Danny, it's okay. Listen to me and understand something. I love that old canoe more than any possession I own. But it is just that—a possession, a material thing. If it meant saving your life, I would chop it up and burn it in a minute." Hank propped himself up on his elbows. "We can fix that old White Otter. It needs a new skin anyway."

Danny nodded his head, looking down. His father's beard showed streaks of gray. His face showed pain.

Hank dumped out his rucksack and gave it to his son. "Take what of the trail lunch you need. I don't want any food in here. Leave the top flap of the food pack unstrapped. If a bear shows up, he can have the food. If he sticks his head in here, I'll just punch him in the nose." He tried to laugh. Danny handed him his bear whistle.

"Thanks, camper."

Then Danny leaned over and hugged his father, turned and stepped out of the tent without looking back, zipping shut the tent door behind him.

Mike was sitting on his life jacket by the shore, both feet up on a rock. The fire had burned itself out in the rain. Danny loaded two days' worth of trail lunch into the rucksack, and left the food pack open like his father had told him to do. Then, with the rucksack on his back, he dragged his father's heavy canoe across the campsite and down to the lake.

Mike paddled stern, with his right foot propped up on the thwart in front of him. Danny kept the map with him in the bow. Their goal was to find help, even if it meant pushing all the way to North Bay on Basswood Lake—eight portages away. They munched handfuls of gorp and chewed on licorice twists as they paddled. Gray clouds. Drizzling rain. In less than half an hour they reached Yum Yum Portage—two hundred twenty rods, starting with the meanest of all climbs, as steep as any portage trail could be, mud-slicked with rain.

Danny helped Mike out of the canoe to keep his injured foot dry. He handed him his crutch.

"This is what we call crunch time, little brother. You take the bow up first. I'll try to keep the stern off the rocks as much as I can."

Danny checked out the trail. It looked unbelievably steep. "Lemme' know if I'm going too fast for you," he said to Mike.

"I don't think that's going to be a problem."

Danny lifted the bow up and pulled the canoe out of the water. Mike grabbed the stern gunwale and lifted it off the rocks. After a short, level stretch, the trail broke sharply upward—all rocks and roots and mud. No pine needle path here.

Slowly they climbed. Danny slipped and fell once, then again. Mike struggled with his crutch. Already, the canoe, belly down, was taking a beating on the rocks.

"Come on, pull harder, Danny. We'll be here all day." Mike chided his brother. "This part is only about forty or fifty rods. If we can get up on top, it's mostly downhill from there, except for one stretch of muskeg."

Danny groaned and tried to pull harder, sweating, slipping, falling again and again, cutting his knees, legs covered with mud. Halfway up the hill two fresh windfalls, birch, blocked the path. They had probably come down in the storm. "Whadda' we do now?"

"Climb over or crawl underneath to the other side. I'll push, you pull. Get going!" Mike's face showed bright red with exertion as he lifted the stern under one arm, paddle-crutch under the other.

Danny hustled underneath the fallen birch trees. On the uphill side of the white tree trunks, he reached back and grabbed the bow of the canoe. Then he pulled with all his might. Mike pushed and he pulled, and slowly they slid the belly of the canoe across the tree trunks, leaving streaks of navy blue paint on the white bark.

Mike, with his long legs, crawled over the top of the windfalls. And again, ever so slowly, agonizingly, they crawled up and up and up, until finally the trail leveled out—but it had taken them half the morning.

"Danny, we're in trouble." Mike, sounding discouraged, sat down next to his little brother on a moss-covered boulder as they took a break. "Problem number one—this is taking way too long. At this rate, we're never going to get back here by dark with help for Dad. And you and I both know that he can't spend another night in that tent. Problem number two—my foot is way worse off than I thought. I can barely stand up, much less help carry the canoe. I'm in too much pain." Mike looked at Danny. "Do you think you can carry the canoe?"

"What?"

"It's really not any heavier than the crusher pack. It just takes getting used to balancing it."

"I don't know." Danny shook his head.

"You have to try, Danny. You have to try for Dad. Come on. I'll lift it up and you can back into the yoke." Mike stowed the paddles across the bow seat. He set the rucksack and his life jacket aside. Then he limped over to the bow of the canoe and raised it upside-down as high as he could. The stern end pressed against the root wad of a downed balsam fir tree.

Danny backed into the yoke. The pads were spaced for his father's broad shoulders, too wide for him, but his life jacket seemed to help cushion the hard wooden yoke. Mike pulled the bow down, balancing the canoe on Danny's shoulders. The weight of the stowed paddles in the bow matched the weight of the drag-plate across the stern.

"How does it feel?"

"Man, this is heavy."

"Try walking."

Danny stepped onto the portage path and moved forward. "I dunno' about this, Mike."

"Try, Danny, try! Remember wolf-moose-eagle-bear, wolf-moose-eagle-bear. That's how Dad does it. That's how Dad taught me. Put the pain out of your mind—wolf-moose-eagle-bear."

Danny stumbled forward along the muddy path, which had started to break downhill—nine feet of wooden canoe in front of him, nine feet behind him. He knew enough not to let the stern drop down and bang on the rocks behind him.

"Good, Danny, good!" Mike cheered. "Go! Go! Get as far as you can. If you have to stop, run the bow between two birch trees for a canoe rest."

Danny's legs wobbled, and his neck ached unbelievably. "Wolf-moose-eagle-bear," he repeated to himself over and over, not caring what foot went where as he ran, now, with the canoe, alone, crying in pain, careening down the trail with the big blue eighteen-footer on his shoulders, a true voyageur, until wham!—he fell hard onto the rocks.

Mike found him underneath the canoe, scuffed and bruised, but not seriously hurt. "That was fantastic, Danny! Can you do that again?"

Danny nodded his head. "For Dad, yes. For you, no."

"That's good enough for me." Mike helped his brother back into the yoke pads. This time he knew what to expect. Beneath the canoe he thought about his father in the tent on Kahshahpiwi. He had not realized what a heavy burden he had carried on all the portages—making it look so easy.

As Danny trudged through a stand of cedar, the steep downhill trail leveled out for maybe forty yards. But with all his concentration focused on balancing the canoe and on the pain in his neck, he forgot to watch exactly where he was stepping. Muskeg! In an instant he had sunk in deep, up to his thighs with both legs. He was stuck, and the more he struggled, the more the smelly muck sucked him in deeper. The canoe crushed down upon him like a fallen tree. "Mike! Help!" he yelled out, then listened for an answer. Nothing.

Beneath the weight of the wood he suffered until there was nothing left to do but roll the canoe off his shoulders. Splat! It landed belly down into the mud just as Mike came down the trail.

"Ha! Danny, I told you to watch out for this muskeg hole," he laughed. "Come on, moose yourself outta' there."

"No, you get me outta' here!" Danny snarled angrily at his big brother.

"Okay, okay, just let me get around to the other side." Mike worked his way around the pit and pulled the blue canoe, belly down, up onto the trail on the other side of the muskeg. Then he took one of the paddles, reached it out to Danny, and pulled him out of the swampy muck.

"Thanks." Danny was covered with muskeg from nearly his waist on down to his boots. He looked at Mike. "So what are you waiting for? Let's go." Mike again lifted up the bow of the canoe for Danny to back into the yoke.

Wolf-moose-eagle-bear. Wolf-moose-eagle-bear. He carried the canoe another sixty rods, legs straining, shoulders aching, until he found two thin birch trees forming a V, where he jammed the bow. He fell on his knees below the canoe, trying to rub the feeling back into his neck and shoulders. From beneath the canoe he could see that the right gunwale had splintered from his fall on the trail. Would the old White Otter hold up against the rocks?

When Mike caught up again, Danny backed himself into the yoke. Angrily, with a loud groan, he pulled the bow away from the trees and headed down the last leg of the portage, determined to make it to the end. This time he thought about his grandfather—punching that bear in the nose. Fierceness. It was his fierceness that had saved them that night. And it was Danny's fierceness that carried him to the end of Yum Yum Portage.

"Arrggh!" Sliding on the soles of his boots down the rain-slicked rock sloping into Yum Yum Lake, he dumped the canoe off his shoulders with a scream, and nearly fell into the water himself. The boat landed belly down with a splash. He pulled it up onto the rocks, then stood in the lake drinking water from his cupped hands, washing the mud from his torn jeans and the blood from his scraped knees. No other canoe-ists were in sight.

It took Mike a long time to catch up. Danny could see the pain in his brother's face as he hobbled down the trail toward him. But Mike smiled when he saw Danny. "Brother, do you know what you just did? You beat Yum Yum Portage with a wood canoe on your back."

"You can tell it to Mr. Jones, but it feels more like Yum Yum Portage beat me." Danny pushed the canoe into the water. "Get in, and get that foot up." He helped Mike into the stern. "We've lost too much time already." It was almost noon. And so they pressed on, grabbing handfuls of gorp from the rucksack, finishing off the last of their mother's voyageur bars and passing a bottle of bug juice between them.

The next two portages, into Shade Lake, were nothing like Yum Yum; still, they were rugged enough, typical Quetico trails. Danny mostly dragged the canoe. His shoulder and neck muscles had knotted up on him in pain. Across the middle of one portage they followed a channel of water through a black spruce bog, pushing into the muck and muskeg with their paddles. Then Danny dragged the canoe again. Mike tried to help, but he was losing strength. Danny didn't dare pull the tape off his ankle brace to check the wound. He guessed it had bled more with all of Mike's walking.

The gray afternoon wore on. A cold wind blew out of the northwest. Even the wildlife seemed to be in hiding. The route from Shade Lake led them over two very short portages, four rods and eight rods, into West Lake. Still no signs of other campers. The canoe held together. No torn canvas. No leaks. Then, a twelve rod portage took them into South Lake.

At the end of this portage, Danny slid the canoe into the water, pulling it as close to shore as possible. He turned to help Mike, and just at that instant he spotted an osprey, with its brilliant white feathers, swooping down out of the gray sky. The great lone bird extended its claws and pulled out of its dive precisely at the surface of the water where it grabbed a silvery fish and lifted it up into the air—all just a few yards down the shoreline from where he stood with Mike's arm around his shoulder.

Danny was struck speechless at the sight of this, not quite believing what he had just witnessed. But as he followed the path of the osprey up from the surface of the water, he sighted a column of smoke rising up from a campsite just down the lake.

"Look." He pointed.

But at that moment, the tremendous pain in Mike's ankle overtook his entire body. Pressed next to him, Danny could feel his brother's muscles shaking uncontrollably.

"Come on. You're nearly in shock." He took off his life jacket and laid it down in the bow compartment as a cushion for Mike. "You've got to keep warm and elevate your legs."

Mike nodded his understanding of the seriousness of his condition. He let Danny help him lie down in the bow compartment, where the duffer usually sat. Danny lifted both of Mike's legs up over the thwart and across the bow seat. Then he covered his shivering brother with his rain jacket. Next, he pulled out his golden foil emergency thermal blanket. Carefully, he wrapped Mike up in the crinkly sheet to help preserve his body heat. Mike looked pale. Thankfully, the rain had stopped.

"Help is just down the lake. We'll be there soon."

Mike grasped Danny's hand in his. "Thanks, brother."

Danny laid Mike's paddle in the canoe next to him, along with his father's broken paddle, and threw the rucksack and map into the stern compartment. Wading nearly up to his thighs, he pushed the bow around and pointed it toward the campsite down the lake. Then he climbed into the stern seat, his father's place, and began to paddle, steering as best he could into the cross wind.

He was surprised to discover how high above the water he sat in the stern seat compared to the bow, and how difficult it was to keep the long boat moving in a straight line. Equally surprising, as he paddled, relieved to have reached help, he began to sing quietly to himself—his father's favorite trail song:

> "It's the far northland that's a calling me away,
> as take I with my packsack to the road.
> It's the call on me of the forest of the north,
> as step I with the sunlight for my load."

He kept the old White Otter pointed toward the column of smoke as he sang.

chapter ten

RESCUE

About fifty yards down the shoreline from the camp-site Danny began to yell and wave his paddle. "Help! Help!" He too had reached a point of exhaustion, paddling again, then waving and yelling some more.

The campers on South Lake, two men and two women, turned out to be volunteers from the Friends of the Quetico Park organization, traveling in the fall from lake to lake, repairing portages and cleaning up campsites. And by a huge stroke of luck, a Quetico Park canoe ranger had stopped by the site and had decided to camp with the group that night.

They lifted Mike out of the canoe and laid him down on a nylon tarp and sleeping bag next to their campfire, feeding him hot soup. The ranger was equipped with a two-way radio. He called park headquarters, requesting two air ambulances—one to take Mike immediately to a hospital, and one to pick up Danny and fly him back to Lake Kahshahpiwi to find Hank.

While waiting for the float planes, Danny made sure the volunteers understood the special importance and value of his father's wooden canoe—how important it was to send the canoe back on the plane with Mike. The group assured him that they would take care of this for him. They told him that they were on their way to Kahshahpiwi; and they offered to clean up the Forester's campsite and collect any gear that was left behind.

Danny stood by the fire, sipping hot soup from his sierra cup and trying to dry his wet jeans. One of the campers offered him a dry pair of socks, but he shook his head no.

Mike looked better. The color had returned to his face. "I'm gonna' be okay." He looked up at his little brother.

Danny handed Mike his paddle, the one with the moose pictograph painted on it. "Don't forget this."

"Do you want me to take yours, too?"

"No," Danny answered, "I want to keep it with me." Holding the shaft of his paddle, he looked down at the blade where his father had painted the pictograph image of a bear.

They discussed what to do with their father's broken paddle, and decided that Hank would want it in the fire—a fitting end for the wedding gift from their mother that had seen so many lakes and so many campfires. Carefully, both sons took hold of the old paddle and laid it on top of the fire.

Then from behind him, out of the northeast, Danny heard the drone of an airplane engine. He looked up and saw the yellow air ambulance drop down out of the clouds—a single engine float plane. The campers had built up a huge fire by now. Their position on the lake was unmistakable.

The small plane leveled out, skimmed across the waves, set down and taxied toward shore. But Danny didn't wait for

it to land. He grabbed his paddle and the map of
Kahshahpiwi, waded out into the water and climbed up onto
one of the plane's pontoons. And just as the paramedic
pulled him in through the door, he caught a glimpse of a
second yellow plane also dropping out of the clouds to the
northeast. He knew then that Mike would be all right.

"My name's Danny Forester. I'm twelve years old. My dad
has two broken legs. He's lying in a tent at this campsite on
Kahshahpiwi." He showed the pilot the exact spot on the
map that Hank had marked with a big X.

The pilot nodded her head. "Not much daylight left. Let's
go! Fasten your seat belt!"

Danny buckled himself into the passenger seat. And for
the first time all day he let himself feel the worry he held in
his heart for his father, but he didn't want to cry in front of
the pilot.

They taxied back out onto the lake, and then, bouncing
against the waves, took off into the wind. It seemed to Danny
that they barely cleared the tree tops as the pilot dipped the
right wing and turned the plane north toward Kahshahpiwi.

In about fifteen minutes they flew over the whole route
that had taken Danny and Mike a long hard day to cover.
And there, over the dark, cold-looking lake, with just enough
light left in the sky to land and take off again, Danny spotted
his father's red tent.

"There!" He pointed for the pilot to see, shouting above
the noise of the engine. "Down there!"

The pilot circled her plane tightly into the wind and
dropped down sharply, leaving Danny's stomach behind. He
gripped the door handle. When they landed he was the first
one out of the plane, running up into the campsite. The
paramedic followed, carrying a huge orange first aid kit.

"Dad! Dad!" Danny tore open the door to the wrecked tent.

Hank lifted his head and smiled weakly. "Hey, camper, I knew you could do it. How's Mike?"

"He's okay. He's on his way to the hospital in another plane."

"Good man."

The paramedic crawled into the tent alongside Danny. "Mr. Forester, how are you feeling?"

"Could be better." Hank winced in pain.

"All right then, let's get you outta' here. We'll start you on an I.V. in the plane, but first here's a shot of some pain medication for you."

The pilot brought in the stretcher from the plane. Together they strapped Hank in and carried him back down to the floating yellow ambulance. In his hands he gripped his sketchbook and collection of Robert Service poems.

"Looks like someone did a terrific job splinting your legs." The paramedic examined Hank's injuries. Hank pointed to Danny, who was following alongside the stretcher lugging the first aid kit. "Amazing kid you got there."

"I know," said Hank.

Then, wading knee deep in the lake, just as the pilot and paramedic were sliding the stretcher with his father into the rear section of the plane, Danny turned and ran back up toward the tent.

"Hey, kid, forget the gear." The pilot shouted after him. "We gotta' get going."

But Danny didn't stop. Inside the tent he found the treasured old cook kit, and made sure he had the canvas bag and all the pieces together, which he gathered up into his arms and ran back with to the plane. The food pack would be left behind for the bears—as a kind of offering.

Back up in the air, Danny knelt beside his father in the rear section of the plane.

"Look here." Hank opened up his sketchbook and handed it to his son. It contained page after page of sketches of bears. "When we get back home, I'm going to start a series of bear paintings. I know what to paint now."

"Good man." Danny growled a friendly bear growl and handed the sketches back to his father. Then he peered out the window of the plane, downward at the dark Quetico wilderness below.

"What are you looking at?" Hank asked.

"Oh, I was just trying to see what route we might take next year." Danny turned and met his father's eyes.

"Good man." His father growled a friendly bear growl. "Good man."

the end

About the Author and Illustrator

EARL FLECK has canoe camped for thirty years in the BWCAW and Quetico wilderness regions. A psychologist in private practice, and an investigator for the Minnesota Attorney General's Office, he lives with his family near Minneapolis, Minnesota. This is his first book.